Other books by L.B. Shire

To Tame a Wild Heart
Trail To My Heart
For The Love Of a Horse (Lena's Story)
Jeez...My Horse has Long Ears!

CHAPTER ONE

Dustin stared out the airplane window. A thick screen of gray hid any views from sight. The dense gloomy clouds reminded him of an unyielding shield. He closed his eyes and rested his head against the seat's backrest.

Sleep remained elusive. So much had happened in the last seventy-two hours, and rest wasn't one of them. His guts twisted and lurched with the plane's sudden jolt. Anxiety gnawed at him, making him edgier than a caged coon. He squirmed in his seat, unable to get comfortable.

"Please remain seated and buckle your seat belts. The plane will land in five minutes." A woman's strict voice radiated from the loudspeaker.

Dustin's heart pounded like a rhinoceros running on parched earth. A thin sheen of perspiration dotted his forehead as he wiped clammy hands against his jeans. The landing of this plane held a significant meaning. He would be starting over. The beginning of a new life with a man he'd never known, and hadn't given much thought to, until a few days ago.

Black dots danced before his eyes. Painful memories of the days past rushed forth. He clenched his jaw, pushing these flashbacks to the farthest recess of his mind, willing the numbness holding him captive these last hours to return and relieve his grief.

He would not cry, instead he tucked in his chin and willed away the images of those last moments with his mother in the hospital room. His throat tightened as a vision of her pale features flashed in his mind. "No, no, no." He slammed his fist into his thigh.

What is done—is done. There would be no changing his plans now. In minutes, he'd be meeting his biological father. A total stranger. A guy his mother rarely bothered to mention through the years, other than to give him a handful of excuses for his absence.

Dustin took a deep breath to prepare himself for meeting this man. Would he recognize him? Would there be joy on his father's face or inconvenience? Dustin wasn't sure what to expect but figured things couldn't be any worse than they already were. The new life he'd promised himself in the hours since his mother's passing awaited him.

Dustin followed a steady line of passengers down the jet bridge and into the arrival hall. He gripped his carry-on holding the only possessions his grandmother had allowed him to bring, until his fingers ached from the strain.

Distracted, he searched the crowd. He used numbness like a shield to protect himself from the fear threatening to consume him. Families reunited before him with hugs and shouted greetings. He gritted his teeth and continued forward, indifference, his secret weapon.

A quick scan of the lobby brought his attention to the far-left corner. There stood a gentleman dressed in dark jeans, dusty boots and a cowboy hat, holding a sign with the name 'Dustin' written in bold, black script. With a shaky breath, Dustin took a step forward. This man, his father, grabbed the faded hat from his head and held it at his side.

Dustin walked closer, taking in every inch of his dad. He noted with surprise, they shared the same sky-blue eyes, which he looked into every day in the bathroom mirror. The older man's face, brown and weathered, sported a few wrinkles along his forehead. A handlebar mustache couldn't hide the slow smile widening on his lips.

"Dustin? Is that you, boy?"

Dustin nodded. Unable to speak, his tongue was as heavy as a brick against his teeth.

"Good to see you, son." The man pulled him into a bear hug.

Dustin inhaled the unfamiliar scents. His dad smelled of leather with a hint of something he couldn't put his finger on. Something fresh and clean.

"Let me look at you." His father held him at arm's length.

Dustin thought he caught the glistening of tears in the man's eyes.

"I can't believe it's really you." His father pulled a kerchief from his back pocket and took a swipe at his eyes.

"My name's Trent. Since we don't know each other real well yet, you're welcome to call me this. My hope is someday, I may have the privilege of you calling me dad. But we'll save that conversation for a different time."

Dustin nodded and breathed a sigh of relief. It was true, he didn't know this guy. And the thought of calling an unfamiliar person, no matter how similar they looked in appearance, dad, put a bad taste in his mouth.

"We better get on the road. The ranch is a couple hours from here, and I still have horses and chores to tend to." Trent turned on his boot heel and walked toward the exit sign.

Dustin stared at the ground while his father walked away. A cold dose of reality hit him like a splash in the face. The deep-seated fear he'd fought earlier returned to plague him.

Trent paused in midstep and glanced over his shoulder. "Come on, son, everything's going to be okay."

Dustin swallowed. He straightened his shoulders and took a step forward, eyes straight ahead. Nothing in life would ever be *OK* again.

***

Trent stopped at the door. The poor boy appeared exhausted, scared and just plain whipped. His own shoulders sagged under the fatigue of all the life-changing events having occurred the last few days. The news of Holly's death, and Dustin coming to stay at the ranch, passed through him like a raging storm.

The tragic and unsettling phone call from his ex-girlfriend's mother still rattled him. She'd ranted how her daughter had passed away, and his son, *his* boy, refused to return to his private school. Well, what kid would feel up to returning to school immediately after a death in the family? He was still in shock that she would even suggest such a thing.

He didn't know his ex's parents one lick, but he wondered about their judgment regarding the boy. To this woman, it was unacceptable for her grandson to miss any amount of school. Dustin, she stated was given an ultimatum: the private boarding school or be shipped to his father. *Looks like I turned out to be the better choice.*

Trent had never seen his boy before today. He'd decided long ago to let bygones be bygones. He couldn't blame the boy's mother, Holly. They met right after his discharge from the military. He'd started a new career riding broncs on a rodeo circuit. They'd shared a whirlwind romance, with lots of exciting times, but when reality set in, she couldn't live his gypsy lifestyle.

Rodeo was a hard life: full of continuous travels, lots of partying, broken bones, big payouts to nights with an empty belly. At the time, Trent thrived on the wildness of it all. He couldn't imagine settling down to a cozy life in the suburbs, mowing his lawn and reading a Sunday newspaper. So, he and Holly parted ways without so much as a goodbye, only several short months after their meeting.

Nine months later, Holly, sent him a brief note and a birth announcement. A formal letter was included, stating they'd created a son during their short time together. Holly named him Dustin, and Trent would not be liable or responsible for the care of this child. He would not be granted any parental rights, and if he chose to fight this, her father would battle him in court until Hades froze over.

The thought of a child and the added responsibilities scared Trent at the time. His friends all scoffed and said the kid probably wasn't his. But deep in his heart he knew this child, was his flesh and blood.

"Excuse me, sir." A woman dressed in a dark business suit and heels, pulling a large carry-on bag, gave him an irritated glare as she walked past.

"Sorry, ma'am." He grabbed his hat from his head and placed it over his chest, stepping out of the woman's way. Dustin remained beside him, a blank and far-away look in his sorrowful eyes.

"You hungry?" he asked the child.

Dustin looked at him before lowering his gaze.

"No," the boy mumbled and crossed his arms over his chest.

Trent held in a sigh. He wasn't good with kids. Had never been around them. Best to treat the boy like one of the many wild horses he worked with at the ranch. Give him some space and let him come to him when the time deemed right.

"Okay then, to the truck we go."

CHAPTER TWO

Dustin stared out the windshield of his father's pickup truck, watching the wipers try to keep up with rain pummeling the glass like an angry mob. His dad had to hand crank the side window open so a slit in the top would let the air in. "To prevent the windshield from fogging," he'd explained.

Trent turned a knob on the radio to a country station, but kept the volume low. The cab remained otherwise silent. Every so often, Dustin would cast a quick glance in his father's direction. He knew he should make some effort to speak to the man, but words refused to form on his lips.

Instead, he feigned interest in a game on his phone. But this was a ruse, really, he kept himself focused in the deep dark recesses of his mind. A safe place to escape these last few days.

The hum of the engine and the warmth inside the cab made him drowsy. His head bobbed, and eyelids drooped with fatigue. Helpless to fight it any longer, he let himself drift into a deep, dreamless sleep.

"We're here."

The cheery burst of Trent's voice jolted him awake. Dustin leaned forward against the seat belt and wiped the grit from his eyes. He focused on the landscape outside the pickup's window. Here? Where was here? he wondered, staring off into the distance.

A two-story white farmhouse loomed before them.

"Come on out and meet my employers. The owners of the Old Bay Mare Ranch. They are also two of my closest friends. You'll love Mrs. Smith, she likes to be called Betty. This woman makes some mean chocolate chip cookies."

The mention of food had his stomach rumbling. He couldn't remember the last time he'd eaten a solid meal. Dustin obeyed his dad and slid out of the truck, shutting the door behind him.

Taking a step and twisting to the side to work out the kinks in his back, he watched as a black-and-white dog raced to his feet. The dog planted itself in front of him, sitting on its haunches. His bushy tail thumped in rhythm against the damp ground.

"That's Tilly," Trent said with a smile. "She pretty much runs this place and keeps everyone in order. Don't ya, girl?"

Dustin reached down and stroked the dog's soft fur. He'd always wanted a pet. His mom never allowed it. Said pets were smelly and bad for people with allergies. He didn't have any allergies he was aware of. He had never given it a second thought, until now.

"Dustin, would you like to come inside for

some milk and cookies?" A woman's kind voice asked.

He glanced up. Mr. and Mrs. Smith both smiled at him.

"We see you've met our Tilly," Mrs. Smith said, her grin widening as she tucked a strand of gray hair behind her ear.

He stared into the lady's tanned face. Fine lines were etched into her skin, but added to the friendly demeanor which radiated from her. So unlike his own grandmother, whose face reminded him of plastic wrap and whose lips never raised an inch above a thin line.

Mr. Smith stepped forward, hand extended. "It's a pleasure to meet you, Dustin. You can call me Bill if you like."

Bill had a jolly voice and sounded genuinely excited to meet him.

He relaxed and shook the man's calloused hand.

"Nice to meet you both. And, yes please, I would love some cookies." He warmed to Mrs. Smith's question.

The woman reached for his hand, hers warm and rough against his own. Together they walked through the front door of the house. The inside smelled of fresh baked cookies as promised. Dustin's eyes were drawn to the room's walls. Large, beautiful paintings and framed photographs of horses and cowboys covered the faded floral wallpaper. Multiple stacks of magazines, all horse themed, lay piled against the sofa in front of a cheery, crackling fire.

"Have a seat." Mrs. Smith pointed to the sofa and left him, hurrying into the next room.

Dustin walked to the couch and sat down. A comfortable heat radiated from the fireplace, and he reclined into the cushions. More horse books littered the coffee table in front of him.

"Here you are, son." Mrs. Smith smiled and set the tray down. "It's been a while since we've had a youngster at the ranch. I hope you'll enjoy it here. There are lots of things for a young man to do."

Dustin reached for the cup of steaming hot chocolate. He brought the mug to his nose and breathed in the sweet chocolaty scent. "Will I get to ride a horse?" He had wondered the whole trip to the ranch how many horses his father may own, and if he would be allowed to handle and help care for them.

"I'm sure we can work something out. I bet your father's planned something special for you." The woman smiled and winked at him.

"How are we getting along in here?" A booming voice rang out.

Dustin glanced up. His father and Mr. Smith both stepped into the entryway, removing their cowboy hats from their heads.

"He's resting with a mug of my specialty hot chocolate. There are cookies on the coffee table. Anyone like a cup of coffee? I was just heading back into the kitchen." Betty stood and disappeared into the next room.

"I could sure use one," Trent called out, hanging his hat on the coat rack and stepping into the living room."

Dustin listened to their interaction with rapt attention. There was so much to take in, he was unsure where he fit into the scheme of things at this place.

"Dustin, would you like to take a tour of the ranch? Visit with the horses?" his father asked. A wide grin covered his face under his thick mustache.

Excitement built in the pit of Dustin's stomach. He wanted to see the horses. The beautiful animals had always fascinated him. His mother quickly squelched any dream of him ever owning one. *"Horses are dangerous beasts, not to be trusted. I won't have you near one,"* he remembered her saying.

"I'd like that," his response laced with all the calmness he could muster. He sat quiet while the adults discussed the following day's chores, some items needing purchased on the next trip to town, and care of the horses.

"When you boys are done showing Dustin around, come on in for some dinner," Mrs. Smith called.

"Will do," Trent replied, already at the front door pulling his jacket on.

Dustin followed several steps behind the two men. Tilly soon joined them and fell into step beside him. He reached down and stroked her head, and she wagged her tail faster, nudging him with her wet nose.

Their first stop was the barn. As they stepped inside, Dustin felt the temperature grow warmer and the air held the scent of cedar shavings and hay. Several horses called out greetings as they made their way down the aisle.

"These two are Turpentine and Blue. They're both mustangs in training," Trent explained. "All Bill's horses on this spread are mustangs. He likes to keep an eye out for the three strikes mustangs. They are the wild ones who no one adopts after three attempts to home them by the BLM. We bring them to the ranch and train them, before finding them new homes.

We have ranches all over the country who purchase them from us once they're trained. They're hardier, smarter, and just plain tougher than the normal horse." Trent stopped in front of Blue's stall and rubbed the horse's speckled face.

"Some of the other mustangs living on the ranch are ones we've brought in from troubled situations. A couple of our most recent additions are horses whose owners passed on, and they had nowhere else to go."

Dustin listened in awe. He wanted to step closer to the horse, to run his hand down his soft shoulder, but fear kept him paralyzed in place.

"Son, you know much about horses?" Mr. Smith asked.

Dustin shook his head. He didn't know much

at all, thanks to his mother's protective streak.

"That's okay. It won't take you long to get the hang of things. Horses are in your blood. Your daddy here can take a wild pony and turn it into a well-mannered ranch horse in no time at all. I have never seen anything like it."

Dustin gazed at his father in wonderment. The man's eyes were hidden under the brim of his hat, so he couldn't read his expression.

"Dustin, follow me. I have a surprise I've been dying to show you since the moment I picked you up from the airport."

Dustin's heart plunged into panic. What did he mean by surprise? There were enough surprises thrown at him in the last couple of days to fill-up a lifetime. His mother's passing, the trip to this ranch. His mind raced as he broke out in a cold sweat, and a wave of dizziness overtook him. He took several deep breaths to steady his nerves.

The last bombshell launched at him was his grandparent's bizarre ultimatum before he left California. Stay with them and live by their rules, which included: returning to his private school for the summer and receiving his mother's trust money early, or going to live with his father and delay the funds until he was of college age. He didn't even care about money. What more could these adults spring on him?

Squaring his shoulders, he stared into his father's face. "Okay," he said, trying to sound brave, but the words came out more of a squeak, like a scared mouse on the run.

"Follow me." His father turned on his boot heel and headed toward the opening at the farthest end of the structure.

Mr. Smith gave him a wink and a lopsided grin, his brown eyes twinkling. He clapped a comforting hand on Dustin's back and directed them after his father.

The opposite entrance opened to a spacious fenced meadow. The grass grew green and lush over the gently sloped terrain. A gentle breeze blew against his cheek as his gaze homed in on a lone horse. The animal stood tall and proud against the backdrop, his dark mane and tail fluttering in the breeze. The horse remained motionless, facing the mountain peaks in the distance as if they were a beacon, he didn't want to lose sight of.

Dustin's father let out a shrill whistle. The mustang cocked an ear in their direction, then forward again. The steed shook his gallant head and pawed the earth with his hoof. In one fluid movement, the horse turned and thundered toward them. His muscles rippled beneath his reddish-brown coat. The animal came to a sliding stop several feet before them and bobbed his head.

"Hey, boy. Look who I brought home." Trent grinned.

The horse looked at them, eyes bright and curious, ears alert. His nostril's flared as he breathed in their scents.

"Dustin, this is Scamp." Trent stepped forward and placed a hand on the horse's neck.

"Scamp, meet your new owner, Dustin."

His father clamped a warm hand upon his shoulder.

Dustin let out a shallow breath, hands trembling. *Could it really be true?* He peered hard at his father. His mother would never allow for this. Tears formed in his eyes, and his vision blurred. His mother was no longer here to say any different, and this knowledge cut through his heart. Unable to handle the turmoil building in his soul, he did the first thing that came to mind. He ran.

***

"Oh boy, what have I done?" Trent's heart sank. He rubbed his temples as his son disappeared into the distance. Maybe the boy hated horses? Had his mother jaded his view of the creatures? He'd hoped by giving the boy a gift, they'd have a connection. Something to bring them closer together.

"Don't be hard on yourself, Trent. The boy's struggled through a lot the last couple of days. Give him time to adjust. I saw the light in his eyes when you told him about the horse. The love is there."

Trent nodded and continued to rub the silky-smooth hide on Scamp's shoulder. The mustang arched his neck, his soft nose poking at Trent's chest pocket. "No treats right now, Scamp, ole buddy."

"I'll go find the boy and have the missus put some spoiling on him. You finish the chores out here." Bill slapped Trent on the back. "Tomorrow's a new day. You and your son are going to get along just fine."

CHAPTER THREE

Dustin ran until his legs felt like rubber. When he glanced over his shoulder, only grass and mountain ranges loomed in the distance. He dropped to the ground, ignoring the sharp pain in his knees as he skidded across the raw earth. Tilly followed, her tail thumping against his back. He struggled to catch his breath: the air held a bite and his lungs burned from his escape.

He stared into Tilly's doe brown eyes. The dog licked his cheek and pressed her moist nose against his chest. Dustin hugged the animal close, his damp face sticking to her soft fur. Why did his mom have to die? His shoulder's shook, anger and sadness battled inside him as his tears fell. "Not fair, not fair, not fair," he chanted under his breath.

Moments later, he heard footsteps behind him. Tilly raised her head and wagged her tail.

"Dustin, why don't you come inside?" Mrs. Smith suggested, her voice soothing.

"It's getting late. Dinner's ready, anyhow. A little warm food in your belly will make things better. After you're through eating, we'll get you settled in for the night." The older woman placed a comforting hand on his back.

He didn't answer. How can she understand? She doesn't know anything about me. He stood, brushing the dirt from his pant legs. His stomach betrayed him with a loud rumble, and his mouth watered with the thought of food.

"We're so glad to have you here, Dustin. And your father, well, one would have thought he'd won the lottery when he found out you wanted to join us at the ranch." The woman paused mid-sentence.

When he peered into her face, her smile widened. "It means a lot to Bill and me to have you staying with us. We haven't had a child here in so many years..." Her voice held a tinge of sadness.

Dustin didn't know how to reply to this. "Thank you," he said. It seemed the most polite response.

They walked in silence through the front door of the ranch house. The smell of roasting meat and fresh baked bread raised his spirits. He was hungrier than he thought.

"Go wash up, the rest room's off to the left." Mrs. Smith pointed. "There's a clean hand towel on the counter."

Dustin walked to the sink. The warm water from the faucet burned his skinned palms. He gazed at his dirt-streaked, tear-stained face in the mirror. His face was still puffy from earlier. Something caught his attention though while he focused on his features. Something he remembered from the past. The blue in his eyes matched the color of his father's. To a T.

He leaned in and stared harder. The curve of his jaw, the shape of his nose. All his father's. This knowledge calmed him. The only characteristic he recognized from his mother were the annoying freckles dotting his cheeks, and the slight oval contour to his ears. Definitely his mother's ears, he decided.

Refreshed and in better spirits, he returned to the dining room. His father sat by Mr. Smith. Mrs. Smith pulled a chair from the table at her side. Dustin managed an uneasy but polite smile for the benefit of the group and sat down. He pushed himself to the table and went to reach for the platter of bread.

"Hold on, son. We say grace in this family," Mr. Smith piped up, winking at him.

Dustin rested his hands on the table. "Sorry," he muttered, his face warming. In his mother's home, there were no such formalities.

After a short prayer, Mr Smith looked at him and smiled. "Dig in, Dustin. There's enough here for a whole passel of cowpokes."

Dustin reached for the platter once more, filled his plate with several rolls and passed the dish on to Mrs. Smith.

"This is a mighty fine dinner, Betty. Thank you again," Trent complimented.

"As always, you're welcome." Mrs. Smith turned a shade of pink with the flattery.

The rest of the dinner conversation went between ranch chores, cattle prices, and horses. Dustin listened, but once he finished his meal, his eyelids started to droop. The warmth of the room, food in his belly, and overall contentment made him drowsy.

"Looks like someone could use some rest. Follow me, I'll show you to our bunkhouse." Trent gently shook his shoulder.

Dustin's curiosity was awakened. "We live in a bunkhouse?" Images of a small room, sporting bunk beds and a cheery fireplace, came to mind. Something like you'd see in an old western on television.

"A mighty fine one, too. It's really just a small cottage house though, but I liked the term *bunkhouse* better," his dad answered. "I put your belongings in there earlier. Why don't you go brush your teeth and crash in bed? Morning comes early around here." His father grinned.

Dustin followed behind his dad along the well-worn path. The trail led them to the back of the main house and into a grove of trees. There stood a modest house with a covered porch, complete with rocking chair parked by the front door, to greet them.

"Welcome to our humble abode." Trent opened and held the door for him.

Dustin stepped inside. A single table lamp cast a warm glow over the small living room. The only furniture was a sofa off to the right, a glass topped coffee table littered with magazines, and a leather lazy boy.

"Your bedroom's to the right. Mine's on the

left. We share the bathroom in the middle. Go check it out. Betty came in earlier, making sure everything looked perfect."

Again, Dustin's emotions threatened to overflow. His vision blurred, and he swallowed hard to keep tears at bay. He'd never been a crybaby, so why start now?

"I appreciate all you've done for me," he managed to squeak out.

"You're welcome, son. I figure, I have lots to make up for. But, we'll start small and take each day as it comes."

Dustin nodded and walked toward his room. Inside the doorway, he felt along the wall until he found the light switch and flipped it on. A twin bed covered in a bright blue and red quilt set against the far side of the space. His backpack lay against the pillow. The dresser sat in front of a large picture window to the left of his bed. He would be sure to check out the view first thing in the morning.

Energy waning, he flipped the light off and lumbered to the bed, kicking off his shoes and tossing the backpack to the floor. He pulled back the quilt, liking the weight of it. Hopefully, his dad wouldn't be angry, but there was no way he was getting out from under these covers to brush his teeth tonight. He fluffed the pillow and rested his head into its feathery softness. He closed his eyes and drifted into the darkness.

***

Trent lingered until he could hear soft snores

before walking over and shutting Dustin's bedroom door. Though bone-tired himself, his thoughts raced on. His son was here...with him. He'd waited anxiously over the last several days for this moment. What a shame, he thought, suddenly weary. It took Holly's passing for the two of them to come together.

He could tell Holly had been an exceptional mother, by Dustin's good manners. He could also see the boy lacked confidence in himself by the continued glances of worry the child threw his way when he thought Trent wasn't watching.

He couldn't blame the kid though, he harbored his own self-doubts. Could he make a good father? He had never spent much time around children before. Horses and cows and the quiet serenity of the hills were his life for all these years. This question had haunted him all afternoon.

Trent hung his hat on the coat rack and headed for the kitchen to make himself some coffee. He fidgeted around the small space while the coffee pot worked its magic. After pouring his cup, he walked to the living room and sat in the recliner. He pulled the string on the table lamp and stared into space, drinking his brew.

He didn't own a television. No need or desire for one. He preferred his life uncomplicated, so he did without many of the modern conveniences of the day. These 'things' had not been missed in his life.

Should I get one for the boy? He was probably

used to watching movies, most kids were. Along with video games. On the drive to the ranch, Dustin never let loose of his phone once. Silent and brooding, he had remained fixated on his screen, fingers tapping the small device with practiced precision.

Trent didn't own a cell phone neither. His son would be disappointed when he realized the service was spotty at best on the ranch. There were some areas where he rode searching for cattle, mending fences, and doing what ever other chores needed doing, that there was none.

He did own an old-fashioned telephone, attached to his kitchen wall. Betty always teased him about his dinosaur of a phone. It was the kind you had to remove the handset from the base to place a call. You actually needed to place your finger on the number you wanted to dial, then rotate the dial clockwise for each number. It worked perfectly for his needs. He rarely used this one, having shut himself off from the world years ago.

He stifled a yawn. All these thoughts of 21st century technology made him sleepy. He put the cup down and stood, ignoring the creaks and pops in his joints with the movement. With one last glance around the room he headed for his bed. Tomorrow would bring forth a new day. A day with his son.

CHAPTER FOUR

Dustin opened his eyes and stared at the ceiling. In his dream, he recalled hearing a noise similar to a rooster from a cartoon he watched when he was younger. The alarm sounded again from outside his window. This wasn't his imagination, he realized, there must be a real rooster outside the bunkhouse.

He leaped out of bed and braced himself against the windowsill. The sun's rays warmed him through the glass. Sure enough, a cocky, red feathered bird strutted across the yard before stopping, careening his neck toward the sky and letting out another call for morning wake up.

Dustin rubbed the sleepies from his eyes. A loud clank and rustling noises outside his bedroom door caught his attention. He left the window and walked out to see what his father was doing.

"Morning, son. Care for some coffee?" His father reached for a second cup from the open shelf.

Coffee? He had never been allowed to drink coffee before.

"Sure." He shrugged his shoulders. "Sounds good." He pulled the chair out from the table, then sat down and waited. His father set the steaming beverage in front of him. The aroma perked his senses. He grasped the cup in his hands and lifted it to his mouth. The hot bitter brew singed his throat on the way down. He coughed and sputtered, his lips curling.

"That's some stout brew. Should put a dash of cream and sugar in there to sweeten it a bit. I don't have any here, but Betty's sure to have some in the house. Let me go grab you some."

"No. It's okay. Really." He wanted his dad to see he was tougher than he looked.

"You want some breakfast?" Trent turned toward the open cabinets on the wall. Rows of boxes in various sizes and colors lined the wooden shelf. He wrapped his hand around an oval container and placed it on the counter. "How about some oatmeal? It's filling and easy to make."

Dustin looked down. He despised oatmeal. A bagel or pastry was more his style. "Sure," he said instead.

Trent grabbed a saucepan from the countertop, filled it with water from the faucet and set it on the stove to boil.

"This will be ready in a minute. I need to get out to the barn and start chores soon. You want to help with the horses or rest a bit longer this morning?" his dad asked, while bringing his coffee mug to his lips.

The coffee was doing its job. Not only did it warm his insides, Dustin figured he'd enough energy to do chores all day long. Though bitter, the brew was growing on him.

"I can help with the horses?" He wanted to learn more about Scamp. The realization no one would take away these animals from him eased his mind. This was Trent's home, and the animals were under his keep. He wouldn't be forced to stay away from them. His mother no longer could tell him no.

"You bet, we'll get started soon as we eat our morning mash." His dad chuckled. "This will give you an opportunity to have a fresh start with Scamp. I'm sorry about yesterday. I didn't mean to push him at you so quickly. I guess horses have a special place in my life, and I wanted to share this with you."

"That's all right. I actually really like horses. Mom would never let me have one or even be near them."

His father frowned, turning his back to him to take the now boiling water from the stove. He poured in some oatmeal and stirred it over the sink, then placed a bowl of steaming mush before him.

"Life will be a lot different from now on. Things don't move real fast here in the country, definitely not a rat race like the city. Every day you'll find new discoveries. I'm getting up in years as you can see by the scattered silvers." He pointed to his hair. "I can honestly say, not a day goes by where I don't learn something new from this place. My hope is you'll enjoy the pace here, maybe learn to love it, like I do."

Dustin nodded. His whole world had been turned upside down the last couple of days. He wasn't sure what he loved at this point. Each day brought a different circumstance along with new adventures. All he could do now was hope for the best. With a horse in the picture, it was looking better and better.

"Chow down, boy. Let's go see some horses."

Dustin scooped a spoonful of oatmeal into his mouth. The quicker he ate, the less he'd dwell on how much he disliked it. Once finished, he pushed his chair from the table and took his bowl to the sink.

"Rinse it out and put it in the dishwasher. Then, better go get dressed. I'll meet you at the barn."

Trent grabbed his hat from its hook on the wall, shoving it on his head and reached for the door handle.

"I'll be out in a sec." Dustin raced to his room to change.

***

Trent pushed the wheelbarrow full of hay down the barn aisle, tossing several flakes of the fragrant grasses to each horse along the way. By the time he'd finished feeding the horses in the barn and started to load the trailer attached to the four-wheeler, Dustin came skipping his way.

"Ever ride on an ATV?" he asked.

"No, sir. Wasn't allowed. My friend, Tommy, had one though. His family used to have a lot of fun out riding trails in the mountains."

Trent patted the fender on the ATV. "This

piece of machinery is a cowpokes best friend when it comes to chores. Hop in the wagon, we'll take this hay out to the pastures to feed the horses. You can start with Scamp. Each horse needs about two to three flakes."

Dustin gripped the hard-plastic siding of the trailer and swung his legs over the rail. He sat down on one of the bales of hay and gave Trent a thumb up.

Trent paused, looking at his son's feet. "You own a pair of boots? Fancy tennis shoes like those won't last long out here in the mud and muck."

Dustin shook his head. "This is all I've got. Other than some sandals and a pair of dress shoes I wore to mom's funeral."

Trent rubbed his chin. "Well, after chores, I say we head into town and get you some proper ranching attire, boots included. How does that sound?"

Dustin smiled. "Sounds good to me."

They finished the morning feeding, Trent driving with Dustin throwing the hay over the fence lines.

Trent sent Dustin into Scamp's pasture. Boy and horse greeted one another. Dustin tossed the horse's hay flakes to the ground and then ran his hand down the mustang's side while the gelding nosed around his breakfast. It warmed Trent's heart to see Dustin coming along so well.

The drive to town was for the most part silent, but a comfortable silence. Trent turned on some country tunes while Dustin doodled on his phone.

"There's some beautiful country here," Trent stated, pointing toward a green pasture full of cattle.

Dustin looked out his side window, a small smile forming on his lips. "I think I can get used to a place like this."

Trent gazed at his son. He held back a grin over the small victory he knew he'd won when Dustin put his phone away to observe the passing landscape. They pulled into the farm supply store minutes later. Trent found an open parking spot near the front of the building, put the truck in park and killed the engine.

"Let's get you some clothes."

Trent walked Dustin straight to the clothing section. "Know what size you wear?"

Dustin shrugged his shoulders and glanced around, a lost look on his freckled face. Trent scratched his head; clothes shopping wasn't his strength. He knew where his jeans and shirts were in the store, but anything other than ranch supplies was beyond him.

"Never mind." Trent chuckled. He browsed through the closest jeans rack. "Here, we'll start with these blue jeans. They're good quality and comfortable to ride in. I wear this brand myself." He handed the boy several sizes he thought might work and walked him to the dressing room. "I'll wait out here."

"Can I help you?" A pretty brunette with long curly hair and a friendly smile approached them.

"Just buying my son some clothes." He liked how the word *son* rolled off his tongue. "We're not sure what size he wears so he's trying on several pairs of jeans. We'll need some boots, too."

"I'll be glad to help. How old is your son?" She gave him a wide smile.

"He's twelve."

"Well the young men's clothing section is over here." She walked several racks over and pulled three pairs of jeans off their hangers.

"These were all too big." Dustin stood outside the dressing room door holding the pants in front of him.

"Here, try these. I think you'll find them more your size." The assistant handed Dustin the more appropriate sizes and stepped back, looking over her shoulder and winking at him.

With the sales associates help, they had all the clothing they needed. A pair of boots, a cowboy hat, some spurs, and Trent couldn't resist the children's size lariat.

All in all, they'd had a successful shopping trip. "You like cheeseburgers?" He asked on the way out of the store.

"Yes!" Dustin's eyes lit full of joy.

"I know just the place." Trent stopped off at a burger joint down the street from the store. They filled up on cheeseburgers and fries then topped off the feast with ice-cream sundaes.

"Thanks, these burgers were great, and I think this is the best sundae I've ever had," Dustin said, licking the last bit of ice-cream from his spoon.

"You're welcome." Trent patted the boy on the back.

Trent couldn't resist looking over at his son on the drive home. The sun highlighted his brown locks through the window. Dustin looked so innocent in his sleep. He turned his attention back to the road. He beamed with pride. His son was by his side.

CHAPTER FIVE

The weeks flew by for Dustin. In the beginning, he'd felt awkward and out of place, no matter how hard he tried to fit in. From tying a safety release knot, to finding Bill the fence post driver, he felt like a fish out of water. Bill reassured him over and over, "don't be so hard on yourself, you're doing a fine job."

The early morning feedings in the wet and cold, shoveling wheelbarrow after wheelbarrow of manure, hefting heavy hay bales around the barn, these chores took their toll. His scrawniness annoying him to no end. Now, he awoke each morning in anticipation. He'd grown tougher, both mentally and physically. Those hay bales didn't intimidate him like before.

His favorite time of the day came after dinner, when his dad gave him a riding lesson on Scamp. With each ride, he grew braver, and more comfortable in the saddle. He'd overheard his dad telling Bill he was a born horseman, with his light rein and solid seat. It helped having an awesome horse, he thought with pride. He'd never loved anything like he loved Scamp.

The next morning as they finished the barn

chores, Trent surprised him.

"Grab your hat, cowboy. We're going for a ride. Outside of the ring today!"

"Are you serious?" Dustin couldn't believe his ears. "Yes, sir!" He ran for the bunkhouse. Just inside the front door, his cowboy hat hung on the coat rack. He pulled it off the hook and shoved it on his head. By the time he'd made it back to the barn, his dad had the horses saddled and ready.

"Today, we'll head out to the mountain. I need to search for a few of the ranch's missing heifers. You feeling ready for a challenge?"

Until now, Dustin had only taken his lessons in the round pen, practicing his skills in the enclosure of the small pasture next to the barn. He swallowed hard, not wanting Trent to detect his apprehension.

"I think so," his words betraying his sudden doubt.

His dad must have noticed his hesitance. "Don't worry, son. Scamp will take good care of you. He was born and raised in this country, and he's a dependable mount to have out there." Trent handed Scamp's reins to him.

"I'm not worried." Dustin smiled and rubbed the mustang's forelock. The gelding brushed against his chest with a soft muzzle in turn. He started to relax. This would be a fun outing for them.

Scamp had become his best friend. Dustin found a kind of peace when near the horse, a calm like he'd never experienced before. Though the mustang couldn't speak, they shared a secret language; a type of understanding between them he didn't know how to explain. In his horse's soft brown eyes, he recognized the quiet strength and determination to move on through any adversity. Dustin had lost his mother, Scamp had lost his freedom and previous way of life when he was captured.

His dad told him Scamp was removed from his home range several years ago. Dustin figured that was why the bay horse stood alert, with his ears cocked toward the mountains each morning when he came out to help feed. He must miss his family, his old way of life, Dustin thought.

Dustin stroked Scamp's shoulder. The mustang turned his head and nuzzled his neck with his muzzle, the horse's velvety lips making him giggle.

"Mount up, let's head on out." His father smiled down at him from atop his horse, Buck.

Dustin gathered Scamp's reins in his left hand, copying his father. He reached for the saddle horn, put his left foot into the stirrup and pulled himself into the saddle. Once settled, he clicked his tongue and Scamp stepped out, into a walk.

"Good job. Keep Scamp behind me. He should follow along easily."

His dad was right. Scamp gave him no trouble at all and he started to relax. They rode in silence for several minutes. Dustin breathed deep, enjoying this time. He loved the scent of fresh pine in the air. A slight breeze tickled his cheeks and rustled Scamp's dark mane.

"Keep an eye out for those heifers. They were probably sidetracked by the pastures on the other side of this mountain. They like to hang out in brambles and thick foliage when they can, for protection."

Dustin scanned the horizon. He didn't see anything resembling a cow. He did notice a hawk against the deep blue of the sky as it swooped low and let out a cry. Otherwise, all was quiet, like observing a landscape painting at the museum his mom used to take him to on rainy days.

The horses weaved through the Ponderosa pines and moved upward into the mountain forests. Dustin watched Scamp's ears twitch forward and back in a rhythm of their own. A movement from the corner of his eye caught his attention.

"Look! Over there." He pointed down the side of the hill. A bull elk and his harem of cows grazed between tall Ponderosas. "They're huge." Dustin had never seen such gallant animals. At least not in real life. They were amazing.

"Bill used to run a guided pack outfit out here in the fall. He would take small groups of hunters camping out in these mountains and they'd all hunt until they filled their tags. We haven't done any trips for some time. Looks like the bulls have grown these last few years. It's nice to see them like this," Trent commented.

Dustin nodded, following the herd's movement. Soon, the animals disappeared from view. The excitement of seeing the elk wore off after a while. They continued their trek through the forest.

Dustin watched amused as Tilly chased the little squirrels in and out of the bushy undergrowth as they rode by. The furry little rodents ran rampant along the tree line running up the trees and jumping from limb to limb. Sometimes they would stand on their haunches, watching them, their chirps loud, to scare off the furry, black-and-white, four-legged intruder. Before he knew it, several hours passed by.

"There's a lake not much farther along the trail here. We'll stop there for some lunch. Betty, I'm sure, packed us a good one."

Dustin's stomach rumbled with the images of food racing through his mind.

Several minutes later, they'd reached the lake. Dustin dismounted, his legs wobbly beneath him. Ignoring the minor discomfort, he dove into the saddlebag, pulling out the insulated lunch bag Betty had packed for them.

"Go sit under the willow tree by the lake while I tether the horses, so they can graze." Trent reached over and ruffled Dustin's hair. He grabbed Scamp's lead rope and walked the horse forward.

"I can't wait to see what she's made for us." Dustin smiled and with Tilly at his side, headed toward the tree.

"There're brownies in here! Holy smokes. And ham sandwiches, pickles, some beef jerky and a sports drink. Betty sure knows how to pack a lunch! I can't believe there's so much food here," Dustin called out, amazed.

"Well, it never hurts to have a hearty lunch. Especially when you're out riding on the range like this."

Dustin bit into his ham sandwich. It tasted better than any fast food he'd ever eaten. "Thanks for taking me on this ride. It's a lot of fun, and I'm feeling more comfortable with Scamp." Dustin quieted and looked at his dad, contemplating whether he should admit how much he loved Scamp. Every night he thanked his lucky stars for the horse. His very own horse.

"I knew Scamp was something special when I found him. He's Ochoco born and bred. There's not a finer mustang around these parts, and I'm glad to see the ole boy bonded so well with you. Once you've gained the trust of a mustang, you will have a friend forever. You were just what that horse needed."

Dustin took another bite of his sandwich, thinking on those words. After a sip of his drink, he lay back on his elbows, taking in the view of the lake. He liked knowing Scamp trusted him. He closed his eyes and smiled, enjoying the warmth of the sunlight and the heat of Tilly's body against his leg.

When he opened them again, he noticed several ducks swimming along the edge of the lake. A colorful green mallard occasionally ducked his head under the water. Each time he surfaced, he would flap his feathers and squawk at the other ducks. For some reason this made him laugh out loud.

"Well much as I'd like to sit here and relax all day, we still have two cows to find. We better get back at it," Trent said, raising to his feet.

"I'm ready." Dustin stood and stretched his arms toward the sky. All the riding he'd done since his arrival had boosted his strength and stamina. He could still recall those sore muscles after his first few days in the saddle. He'd wondered if his legs would ever work properly again or if he would be able to sit in a chair without a pillow to pad his bottom. He'd ached down to his bones. The only way for him to get moving in the morning was the perk from a cup of his dad's cowboy coffee, as he so lovingly called it.

They rode into heavily wooden terrain leading into another prairie thick with lush spring grasses. "I call this heifer haven. What nicer place to disappear to than a valley full of grass with fresh spring fed water?"

Dustin looked around. He agreed, if he were a cow, he would probably search for a place just like this. He crumpled his face with the thought. He couldn't believe his thinking. A month ago, he would have never looked twice at a meadow of grass. Now, his dad had him thinking like a cow. He couldn't help but chuckle.

Scamp pawed the ground, pulling against the reins.

"What's he doing?" Dustin gripped the saddle horn tighter, but soon relaxed when he realized Scamp wasn't going to run off with him.

"Looks like we found our cows." Trent rested his elbow on his saddle horn and pointed off to the left. "Let's fall behind them and push them slow-like back down the mountain. Stay behind me, and let the horses do the work."

Dustin loosened Scamp's rein and took a deep breath to calm himself. The ride home went much slower. Dustin followed his father's lead, pulling his cowboy hat farther down his forehead to protect his eyes from the now glaring afternoon sunlight. When they reached the last pasture before the ranch, the cows spotted the rest of their herd and broke into a run. The heifers mooed their greetings and dirt clods flew through the air as they sprinted for home.

"Let's get the saddles off the horses and brush them out. It should be about time for dinner. I smell something delicious coming from the house," Trent said, nodding toward the ranch house.

"Smells like more chocolate chip cookies to me!" Dustin rubbed his stomach in anticipation. Mrs. Smith made some killer cookies.

Scamp sighed when Dustin ran the curry over his back in small circles like his dad had shown him. He gently brushed over the scar under his dark mane. A tattoo given to mustangs when they enter captivity, his father had told him. He gave Scamp a final scratch behind the ears, chuckling at the mustang's expressions.

"Where's the hoof pick, Dad?" The word *dad* sounded foreign on his tongue but gave him a sense of comfort.

"Should be in the blue brush bucket by the water hose. If not, there are spares in the tack room."

Dustin sifted through the bucket, finding the hoof pick on the bottom. He walked back to Scamp, lining himself parallel against the horse's shoulder and clucked, rubbing the gelding's lower leg. The horse obediently lifted his hoof for Dustin to clean. He scraped out several small pebbles burrowed under the horse's shoe.

"The horse's hooves are very important. Clean them well before and after each ride. A wayward rock can cause pain and lameness, and your horse will be out of service for weeks," his father's words rang in his mind.

"All set?"

Dustin nodded and led Scamp into his pasture outside the barn. The horse immediately trotted to the center of the area and then lay in the grass, rolling over and kicking his legs toward the sky.

Dustin sensed his father's presence behind him. A warm hand clasped his shoulder and he turned to smile at his dad.

"Let's go get some of those famous cookies," Trent said.

***

Trent smiled at Dustin. Today's outing on the range proved rewarding. He loved seeing how his son had matured over the last few weeks. The fresh country air and daily work ethic needed on the ranch was better medicine than any prescribed drug. Trent had always chosen the company of a good horse and a long weekend ride out on the range, over any pills or potions a doctor tried to push at him.

Trent would never consider himself a great father, or even a fatherly figure. No, the time for vying for father of the year had come and past. But now that Dustin was at the ranch, under his wing, he figured he could at least teach the boy about his way of life. And Trent had learned through experience, the best teachers in life weren't always human. Thus, his gift of Scamp to Dustin.

He preferred a simple life. Clean stalls, a barn full of hay, a shed full of firewood and a pantry full of food in his kitchen: this was what he considered a plentiful bounty. Along with a view of the world from the back of a horse. This was all he needed. No bells or whistles, fancy cars or houses one could get lost in for him.

He hoped Dustin wouldn't be put off by his way of life. The boy was accustomed to so much more. Life with his mother, from what Trent gathered by his comments, sounded extravagant. Full of expensive, material things.

Trent didn't like to dwell on his shortcomings. And he didn't feel his minimal way of life shortchanged anyone. If his son wanted more from him, he would try to comply the best he could. He would get the boy a television for the house if he liked, or maybe one of those gaming machines he had mentioned. He would do all of this and more for his son, if he asked him.

Trent had a sneaking suspicion though, Dustin didn't desire any of those things. If he did, he would have asked for them by now. No, from his observations, he figured his son seemed pretty happy with this new life. Dustin was a smart kid and could realize happiness did not always come in a box. Sometimes, joy was found within a living, breathing thing.

CHAPTER SIX

After a hearty dinner, the group sat on the front porch, listening to Bill play his fiddle. Dustin's fingers tapped on the wooden floor in rhythm with the jaunty tune.

"Thanks for playing for us tonight, Bill." Trent clapped, as he stood at the rail looking into the night sky full of stars.

"My treat. I like to play every so often to keep the rust out of my fingertips." Bill chuckled.

"Trent, you should get Dustin off to bed. It's getting late," Betty reminded them, standing up from her rocking chair. "Daylight comes early around here, as we are all well aware." Betty gave them a short wave and pulled open the front door.

"Yes, ma'am. I reckon we better hit the hay." Trent turned toward Dustin and winked.

"Before you go, Trent, Betty and I have a proposal for you. We've kicked this idea around for the last several days." Bill set his instrument down and rubbed his jawline.

"Dustin, head on over to the bunkhouse, I'll be there shortly."

Trent motioned for him to go.

Dustin nodded, but curiosity gnawed at him.

He started to walk away, on the well-worn path to their cottage, but could stand it no longer. He stopped and held his breath in the darkness, hoping to catch a bit of the adults' conversation floating in the breeze.

"A few of the mustangs are needing some back-country experience packing and lead lining before the Bar C Ranch picks them up next month. Thought you might like to take Dustin into the hills for a week with the horses. Might give you two a chance to really connect and get acquainted with each other better."

Dustin closed his eyes and breathed through his nose to steady his heartbeat. What would his father's reply be?

"Let me think it over... he's still green as spring grass, but..."

Dustin jumped into the air and fist pumped. Yes! What an adventure this would be. He ran the rest of the way to the bunkhouse, kicked off his boots at the door and dove into his bed. Clothes and all. Once the covers were at to his nose, he gazed out his bedroom window, watching the stars twinkle in the night sky. He couldn't wait for the next day.

Dustin awoke before daylight. Excitement had him too amped to sleep a second longer. He hopped into the shower and let the warm water wash away the grit of yesterday's ride. After toweling off and dressing, he thought he'd make a good impression by doing their laundry.

Being the bachelors they were, the clothes

tended to pile up until neither of them had any left for the following day. He grabbed the dirty clothes hamper from the bathroom and dragged it to the small laundry room off the side of the kitchen.

Betty had shown him how to use the contraption several days prior. He tossed the clothes in, sprinkled soap on top like she'd instructed him and turned the dial to 'regular.' He walked away proud of himself as the water started to fill the machine.

"Mornin'."

His dad stood in the kitchen, buttoning his western shirt to the collar. The coffee percolated behind him, emitting the strong, wholesome smell of fresh cowboy brew.

"Morning," Dustin replied, while grabbing two bowls from the cupboard. "Oatmeal okay?"

"Sounds like a winner." Trent smiled.

The pantry had grown in abundance since Dustin's arrival. The shelves donned a bit more variety than his first day in the bunkhouse. Now there was an extra can of ground coffee, filters, dried beans, canned chili, some boxes of macaroni and cheese, canned fruit, a loaf of bread, several types of cereal and some crunchy peanut butter. He knew Betty had something to do with the recent additions.

His dad's simple ways were starting to rub off on him. He no longer craved the fast foods and restaurant dinners he was used to. By the end of most days, he was too tired to care much about what was on the menu, whether it be beans and cornbread, his father's standby, or the mouth-watering roasts Betty cooked and invited them over to share.

They sat at the kitchen island and Trent sipped his coffee, real quiet-like, while Dustin took another bite of his hot cereal. He could feel the burning gaze of his father's stare and wondered when he should mention the topic from the night before.

"Care to join me for a little adventure?" Trent's voice sounded a bit shaky and coarse.

Dustin paused mid-bite. "What kind of adventure?" Blood rushed his veins and his heart thundered against his ribcage.

"A mountain trip into the Ochocos with the mustangs. A week at least, two at the longest. We'll be wandering off the ranch and into the wilds."

Dustin finished chewing his food before answering. The thought of riding into the mountains sounded cool, though a small amount of fear nagged at the back of his mind. He'd never camped in his life and camping in the wilderness with horses seemed all the more daunting. And exciting.

"I'd love to go," he finally answered. "Do you think I'm ready for something like this?" He couldn't help but ask. He stared at the floor, wondering how his father would react. Would he be angry at him for doubting he'd keep him safe, or worse, disappointed?

The silence in the room could be cut with a knife while Dustin waited for his answer. Trent pushed his chair back and stood from the table.

Reaching for his bowl, his gaze homed in on Dustin.

"There's no better way to find out than to go out and have a go at it. I'm not saying it won't be hard, or we won't come across any problems. You'll never learn unless you give it a shot. We'll leave on Saturday morning."

Dustin didn't know what to say. He'd the sudden urge to hug his father. He put feelings into action and stood, rushing over and giving his dad a hug. A real embrace. It was the first heartfelt contact they'd had since Dustin arrived at the ranch. His father was all muscle beneath his grip. A warmth flooded him when his dad hugged him back.

Saturday was only two days away. They would need to hustle to prepare for the trip in this short amount of time. Horses needed shod, tack cleaned and prepared, supplies purchased in town. Dustin wondered if there were enough hours in the day to complete all the tasks.

Standing in the shade of the barn, Dustin held the lead rope to Max, a dark colored gelding with grays and white blended together, to give him a blue appearance. A blue roan, his father had called the horse's color.

"Max is a well-behaved boy. He and most of the others here are from the Beatys Butte herd in Eastern Oregon. We purchased Max from a family who adopted him after a roundup. They soon found wild horse training wasn't for them. He's lived at the ranch three months now and is a real fast learner. I've put several good rides on him, and he's calm as can be."

Dustin listened intently while his dad gave him Max's history lesson. "Do you sell all the mustangs on the ranch?"

His father must have noticed the concern in his voice.

"Don't worry, son. Scamp is yours to keep. He'll never be sold."

Dustin let out a silent sigh of relief. "Why's it so hard to find homes for mustangs?"

Trent wiped his forehead with a kerchief and settled on the next hoof. "I s'pose there are many misconceptions about the wild horse. Folk tend to dwell on the bad more often than not. There're a lot of differences of opinions, politics, money, BLM and rancher discontent. In the end, I think the mustangs suffer from it all.

"When you get past all the man-made drama and down to the nuts and bolts of it, I figure owning a mustang is like owning your own small piece of America and freedom. And no matter how small this freedom is, it's yours to keep, protect, and fight for. This, of course, is just my take on things."

Trent, finished now with Max's hooves, sent Dustin off for the next mustang joining in their adventure.

"Easy girl." Dustin put a hand on the horse's shoulder to calm her while he led her past the other horses, watching from their prospective pastures. Arwin was a black beauty, even bearing the white rigid scar from her BLM tattoo.

"Dad, what's Arwin's story?"

Trent rested his hand on her withers. "I don't have much history on this pretty girl. Bill found her at an auction and said he couldn't bear to leave her behind. Don't understand what happens in a person's life to have to resort to those measures. An auction is not a safe place for a horse to land.

"I've worked many a ranch, and with all types of personalities of both men and women alike. Some folk send them to the auctions simply 'cause they don't care, to them, the horse is a material possession, something to be purchased, then tossed away when they no longer have a use for it.

"Others are helpless to control the situation they've been handed in life and feel they have no other option, I guess. I've learned over the years not to judge too harshly. Especially since I don't know a person's lot in life."

Dustin tried to understand what his father said. He mulled the words in his mind but found he couldn't comprehend any of it. All he could hope for was the continued kindness to these gallant creatures his father spoke of here at the ranch. And a hope to never have to leave.

***

Trent found a deep calm in working with a horse's feet. Shaping the hooves, crafting a shoe from steel. It was an age-old art, one he enjoyed practicing. With every horse he shod, he learned something new. He also appreciated the fact his son was so willing to jump right in and help.

Dustin wasn't one of those kids who would sneak away to play video games in the house or sit on the couch watching mindless television shows when there was work to be done. He was proud of his son and how far they'd managed to come in such a short time.

"Son, why don't you give this a try?"

Trent reached for the horse's lead from the boy and handed Dustin his clippers and rasp.

He noticed the worry cross Dustin's face.

"Don't fret none. All cowboys and cowgirls too, should know how to trim their horse, and pull a loose shoe, if needed. The knowledge comes in handy when you're alone out on the trail and your horse throws a shoe. Here, let me show you how to do the first one, and you can try on the next."

Trent showed Dustin what he wanted him to do. "I've said it lots of times before, but a horse's feet and hoof care are one of the most important aspects of horse ownership. Mustangs have good, solid hooves which don't always need shoes.

"Scamp was raised on the terrain we'll be riding through. I'll still put shoes on him, to protect his hooves from sharp rocks. I know some folks who think otherwise, that mustangs don't need the extra protection, but I know I'd rather wear shoes over rocks than try to maneuver barefoot. I reckon my horses must feel the same."

CHAPTER SEVEN

It took Trent and Dustin a whole day to care for the horses and tack that they would be taking on their outing. This left one last day to purchase their food and supplies. On the way to town, Dustin rolled the window down and let the cool air of the early morning wash over his face.

"Son, you ever camped before?" Trent inquired.

Dustin thought back through his childhood. Jumbled memories flashed in his mind. His mother hated anything outdoorsie. They lived in a condo right smack in the middle of the city, so she didn't have to deal with lawns, gardening or house care. She always said she loved her concrete jungle. The only lawn he'd ever laid a foot on was when he visited a friend's house.

"No, can't say I have. Mom always said she worried I would get lost or hurt out in the 'wild,' as she called it. She was afraid I'd be eaten by a cougar or a bear. Jeremy Mackay asked me to go on a camping trip with his family once, and mom almost had a coronary.

"One other time, I asked to go to a wilderness survival camp, cause all my friends were going. She shot that idea down, too. Instead, she sent me to a college camp, where I stayed in a dormitory for two weeks. We did crazy science experiments and made electronic configurations, all day long. It did end up being fun, but at the time I had hoped for a camping trip with my friends."

Dustin turned to see his father's shocked expression. "Don't worry, I think mom meant well. She told me there was a time in her life when she used to love the outdoors, horses, rodeos and all that. She said it was easier and more convenient to read about it in a book or watch it on television, than to do it in real life."

His dad's face turned serious. "I'm sorry your mom felt that way. If it counts for anything, I did ask her to come along with me when we first met. On the rodeo circuit that is. She said it wasn't the lifestyle she wanted to live. She wanted a stable home, job, life." The cab turned silent.

"Rodeo is a hard life. I can't take back the past, but if I could do it over, I'd have tried harder to make things work between your mom and I. She was a special woman."

Dustin warmed to the sincerity in his father's voice, and it soothed a raw area of his heart. There were many questions he wanted to ask his father but hadn't worked up the nerve. Like why he never bothered to see him over the years or make any contact? Why did it have to take his losing a parent for the other to reappear? And why hadn't his mother told him the truth? Instead, she'd sidestepped or flat out refused to answer the questions he'd asked about his father. This hurt.

Dustin remained lost in his own thoughts the rest of the drive to town. When they arrived at the grocery store, he pushed aside his muddled feelings and followed his dad down the snack aisle.

"We need to pack light, but foods with lots of calories to give us energy." Trent grabbed a bag of granola trail mix from the shelf and tossed it into the cart.

Dustin looked at the shopping cart, it was filled with protein bars, instant oatmeal, instant noodle cups, sports drink packets, jerky, and now the granola mix. In the next aisle, they added dried fruit and some canned chili.

"Anything else you might like?" his father asked.

Dustin raised his shoulders. "Looks good to me."

"Let's head over to the sporting goods section and pick out some lures for fishing in the high lakes. Oh, and you'll need a sleeping bag."

His dad led him down an aisle filled with lures of every size and color. "We'll be camping by a few lakes I know for a fact are packed with trout. You'll get to experience some exceptional fishing in those mountains."

"Can't wait." And it was the truth. Dustin had never fished before but had watched men fish on television and thought it looked like fun.

They unloaded their groceries from the cart

into the bed of the truck. On the ride home, Dustin found himself dosing off and on. The long drive and the movement of the vehicle seemed to make him drowsy every time they traveled somewhere.

"We're home. Let's set the supplies on the kitchen counter. We'll be loading them into the panniers the horses will be carrying in the morning."

"What's a pannier?" Dustin asked, reaching in for a grocery bag.

"Panniers are boxes that hang on the sides of a horse to evenly distribute your supplies on their back."

Dustin tried to imagine what this would look like. They had a ton of stuff to put into these boxes the horses would be carrying.

The groceries were soon unloaded and neatly arranged on the counter.

"Dustin, go and pack some clothes. Make sure to grab those wool socks we bought today. You'll need several t-shirts, a wool sweater, jacket, and underwear."

Dustin did his bidding, rolling his clothing tight and stuffing it into a duffel bag. He set the bundle on the floor next to the rest of their supplies and walked over to the living room window. The sound of drawers opening and closing could be heard from his father's room as his dad gathered his belongings. With growing excitement, he paced back and forth while he waited.

"I believe this should do it." His dad came out of his bedroom and tossed his bag next to Dustins.

"Let's get the horses taken care of. Betty wants us to come over when we're through. She's cooked a special dinner for us for tonight."

Dustin raced through his chores. He wanted to have a few extra minutes to spend with Scamp.

"I can't wait for tomorrow, boy." He ran a soft brush down the horse's neck. "Dad says we'll be visiting some of your old stomping grounds. You should like that."

Scamp tickled his neck with prickly whiskers, his soft lips brushing across his cheek.

"Is this some kind of horse kiss?" He giggled and scratched the mustang behind his ears. The horse closed his eyes and relaxed his features, letting Dustin massage the area.

"Dustin, wash up. Betty's waiting on us."

"I'm right behind you," he hollered.

Dustin threw Scamp an extra flake of hay. "See ya in the morning, bud."

Betty outdid herself on the dinner. "I can't believe all this food. It's like a Thanksgiving feast." Dustin stared wide-eyed at the meal spread out across the table.

Dustin shoved his spoon into the large platter of mashed potatoes and filled his plate. There were oven baked rolls, steak, green beans, and his favorite, fruit salad.

"Well, I knew this would be the last home cooked meal you boys see until you return. I wanted to make sure you ate well." Betty smiled and winked at him.

"I have to admit, the food out on the trail may not be four-star, but a bowl of ramen noodles tastes gourmet on a high mountain peak, when you're staring out at the stars at night," Trent lamented.

Bill chuckled at this. "I can't say I would disagree. I recall one trip years ago on the Pacific Crest trail when one of our pack horses spooked and broke away. We searched high and low for the little mustang all through the day. He carried all our camp equipment and food supplies.

"We stopped searching at dark and made camp. That night since there weren't any cooking utensils, we dined on beef jerky and stale biscuits. Those were the best darned biscuits I ever tasted, next to these tonight, of course." Bill looked at Betty and winked.

"Tell me more stories of riding out on the trails." Dustin leaned forward, eager to learn more of these adventures Bill and Trent had taken on horseback.

Bill rubbed his jaw, his brown eyes shined with amusement in the light. "How about I tell you how I got my beginnings? My first pack trip on horseback was when I was around your age, I believe. My older brother Clark and I begged our parents to let us go out overnight with the horses into the woods by ourselves.

"Now, my daddy thought this was a grand idea. He'd done a similar trip himself at our age. My mama was a whole 'nother story."

"These boys are too young, Will," she had argued. "Out gallivanting by themselves overnight in those mountains. It's too dangerous. Let's wait until they're a little older before we let them go."

"I remember the concern in her voice. My brother and I were heartbroken. If mom said no, that was usually the final answer in our house.

"My daddy must have done some sweet talkin' that night, cause the next morning, daddy announced at breakfast that Clark and I should gather our supplies and get moving. 'Your mother expects you back tomorrow evening in time for dinner.'"

"I raided the pantry for our food and Clark prepared the horses. I remember how proud I felt when we rode away from the farm that day. We rode our horses all through the day until we reached a grassy meadow with a pristine lake. We set our camp close by and fished to our heart's content, until we could no longer keep our eyelids open. Yep, I've been trekking into the mountains on the back of a horse ever since."

"Well you boys best get on to bed, you'll need to get an early start in the morning," Betty said, reaching for an empty plate, she started to clear the table.

Dustin beamed. How would he ever sleep tonight? Horses, adventure, the great outdoors! Thoughts of his horse's mane blowing in his face while he gazed over grass covered meadows below him, ran through his mind. No, there wouldn't be any sleeping tonight.

***

Trent sat back in his chair, content with the company and stories they shared. There can be no better life than this, he mused. He'd always preferred simplicity, and there was no greater gift than the sharing of a good horse tale around the table with friends and a hot mug of coffee to warm your hands.

Dustin, he noticed, seemed intrigued with their conversation. The boy had barely gone outside of the house when he lived with his mother. Each day must be a mystery and adventure rolled all into one for him.

Guilt tugged at his heart and a dark shadow replaced the light, happy feelings he had relished earlier. How could he have let himself avoid his son all these years? The boy was a breath of fresh air in his life. A smart, eager, more put together human than Trent had ever been at that age.

He swallowed the last bit of coffee in his mug and pushed his chair from the table.

"Betty warned us earlier, we need to hit the hay. The rooster will be crowing before we know it." Trent stood and turned toward the door. Dustin followed his lead.

"Thanks for the wonderful company. See you folks in the morning." With the last goodbye, Trent ruffled Dustin's hair, and the two walked toward their humble abode.

CHAPTER EIGHT

Dustin heard the telltale 'thump' from the window closing in his father's room and knew his dad had awoken. He swung his legs over the bed and jumped to his feet. He had dressed and readied himself to leave hours ago.

"Mornin," Dustin called out, walking to the kitchen counter to get the coffee percolating.

"You ready for today?" Trent asked, rubbing his mustache as he sat down.

"It's all I could think about last night. I might never have the chance to do something like this again."

He noticed his father's lip twitched with those words. "We'll see about that," he murmured under his breath. "I have another little surprise for you. A small gift, I mean."

"Really? What is it?" Dustin wondered, turning toward his father.

Trent placed a small package on the island. "It's nothing big, but something helpful to have around."

Dustin grabbed the small box and tore open the paper. Inside lay a pocket knife.

"Wow, this is great. I've always wanted one

of these." Dustin opened the knife, examining the blade.

"Thanks, Dad." He grinned at his father.

"No problem. It's one of those things which might come in handy one day. Every man should keep a knife handy. And, it fits easy in the pocket. Just don't forget to remove it before washing your clothes, so it doesn't rust."

Dustin put his new knife into his front pocket. "Fits perfect right here." He tapped his hip.

They ate their breakfast in a comfortable silence.

"We should get moving. Oh, and don't forget your toothbrush," Trent said, raising from the chair.

"Packed and ready." Dustin smiled.

"I love your enthusiasm. Let's go get the horses ready. Grab a bag and we'll start putting our clothing and staples into the panniers." His dad chuckled.

Dustin made several trips, carrying their supplies from the house to the barn, while Trent loaded them into the panniers. The supplies were split up between the two pack horses they would be bringing along, Gator and Arwin.

Gator was a short, stout chestnut mustang with heavily muscled hindquarters. He looked like a hairy mammoth next to Arwin's more delicate build. The solid mustang would replace Max on this trip. Max had cut his leg mysteriously the day before.

"Looks like you guys are ready." Bill walked

forward and ran his hand over Arwin's shiny dark shoulder.

"Should be smooth sailing, weather-wise at least. Betty will be out in a minute. She wants to see you boys off."

Right on cue, Betty stepped out onto the porch, drying her hands on a kitchen towel. She walked forward, stopping at Bill's side.

"Oh, the days of adventuring in the mountains. Bill and I have had lots of good times in those hills," she lamented, a dreamy look on her face. "There is nothing better than sleeping under the stars each night."

Betty stepped forward and placed a hand on Trent's shoulder. "Take care out there. We'll be expecting you toward the end of next week."

"Yes, ma'am," his father replied.

Betty drew him into a quick hug. When finished, she turned to Dustin.

"You're a lucky young man. Not a lot of boys your age get to have this kind of adventure."

Dustin smiled. He did feel lucky.

Betty moved to his side and pulled him close. "Take care, Dustin."

"I will," he said.

Trent had mounted his mustang, Buck, while Betty hovered over him. In his hand, he held the lead line to the two mustangs loaded with their supplies.

"I'm going to camp at the lake tonight. See if we can't catch ourselves some fish for dinner," Trent said, adjusting his cowboy hat on his head.

"There's nothing better than fresh trout cooked over a campfire." Bill patted his stomach.

"Better mount up, young man," Bill said, giving Scamp a rub on the forehead.

Dustin gathered Scamp's reins in his hands and put his boot in the stirrup. He pulled himself into the saddle, arranging himself in the seat.

"Ready?" Trent gave a light tug on the leadline, and Gator, the lead packhorse, stepped forward.

Dustin adjusted his cowboy hat to match his fathers and gave him a nod.

Trent clicked his tongue and the horses moved forward. Dustin fell into place at the back of the line. He turned and looked over his shoulder.

"Tilly..." he hollered. The dog's distinct bark resonated in the distance. Tilly raced around the corner of the house and trotted beside Scamp.

"Good girl," Dustin cooed.

The first hour they followed a well-worn path leading into the mountains. The birds sang from the tree branches when they rode past. By noon, they were heading into switchbacks leading them to higher elevations. A slight breeze whistled through the treetops; chilled, Dustin pulled on a sweater.

"Is this still part of the ranch?" Dustin twisted in the saddle to get a better view.

"Yes, we're at the eastern edge of the property. There's a mountain meadow ahead, and spring fed lake. We'll be there shortly and set our camp for the night."

"This early in the day?"

"Yep. Today will be a learning day, for both you and the horses. It gives me time to monitor how they react to being led on a leadline and how they'll handle being tied to a highline tonight. We'll get them unpacked and unsaddled, then hobble them so they can graze in the meadow for a bit. They've been through all this back at the ranch, but it's different when you're doing it for real."

"What are hobbles?" Dustin asked.

"They're leather bands which we'll attach to their front legs. It gives them a chance to move around while they eat without getting tangled in their ropes. We'll be at the lake in another half hour or so. I'll show you how to set a camp, how to care for the horses and catch our dinner."

They started forward again. As his father mentioned, when they reached the top of the tree line a well-groomed trail led down a sloped hill into a mountain meadow. The lake he'd spoken of sparkled in the distance.

"We'll ride to the grove of trees off to the left of the lake and set our camp there." Trent reined his horse along the trail leading toward the water.

The path grew wider, so Dustin trotted ahead until Scamp was beside Buck. They rode side by side to the lake, then relaxed in the saddle as the horses drank their fill.

"We have special tablets in the pack for filtering the water out here. It's not safe to drink on its own, no matter how crystal clear it may appear."

"Why's that?" Dustin wondered, glancing down at the smooth, glassy surface of the lake.

"There is bacteria in the water from animal droppings. And you never know when an animal may have died near the water source. It can give you the worst case of the drizzles you've ever imagined, if it doesn't kill you."

Dustin cringed at the thought.

"Follow me, we'll get started setting up camp."

The area they chose for the night was in a grove of tall pines. A sweet fragrance lingered in the air as a mild breeze rustled the trees' branches every so often.

They removed the panniers from the mustangs' backs, setting them out of the way. Dustin helped his dad set a highline between two of the trees. Trent pulled two mohair cinches from the panniers. He threw one to him and used his own to wrap around the trunk of a pine. "Protects the bark from rope burns," he offered by way of explanation.

"We need to keep the rope high as a safety measure for the horse. It helps prevent them from getting a hoof or leg caught on the line. It's amazing what kind of trouble a horse can get itself into."

Dustin wasn't tall enough to have the rope the same height as his dad, so he scaled the tree, ignoring the sticky pitch sticking to his fingers and fastened the cord to his cinch. Once his side of the highline was secured, he dropped to the ground. They tied the horses along the line, settling them in.

"Grab a hoof pick and check their feet. Then curry them out and check them for any saddle sores. Horse care always comes first, no matter how tired one might be," Trent stated. "I'll start getting camp ready."

Dustin went through the pannier until he found the grooming supplies. He decided to start with Scamp. The horse dutifully raised each of his hooves while he picked out the loose dirt and rocks. Then the mustang closed his eyes and lowered his head, relaxed, while Dustin ran the curry over his body.

He checked over each horse. "So far so good. No scrapes or bumps that I can see," he called to his dad.

"We'll put the hobbles on them so they can graze in a bit. When you're done there, you can help me get our shelter in place."

Dustin finished caring for the horses. He put the brushes and pick back in the supply pack and replaced it inside the pannier. Tilly nosed around the bag, wagging her tail. "You hungry, girl?" Dustin pulled out her dog dish and a zipper lock bag filled with dog food. He poured some pebbles into the bowl and set it on the ground for her to eat.

Trent pulled a tarp from the pack and laid it flat on the ground. They used rope to attach the top of the tarp to two trees, creating an open-ended tent. Dustin threw their sleeping bags inside, then walked back over to where his dad finished building a shallow fire pit.

"You hungry?"

They'd worked so steady, Dustin hadn't had time to worry about the gnawing in his gut.

"You bet."

Trent grabbed two sandwiches and a bottle of sports drink for each of them. They sat under the pines and stared into the horizon.

"There's lots to learn out here, son. Don't be afraid to ask questions. Tomorrow, our route will take us over some foot bridges, then we'll be crossing a few creeks, and we may run into some snowy passes, too. These mustangs are still green, so we'll take it nice and slow on the trail. Keep things quiet and as stress free as possible."

"Will there be other people out here?" Dustin wondered aloud.

"It's not uncommon to cross paths with other hikers and horseback riders this time of year."

Trent closed his eyes and leaned back against the pine tree. Tilly rested her snout on his leg and closed her eyes, too. "Feel free to take a quick nap. Here in a bit, the fish should start biting. We can head down to the lake with our poles and see what kind of luck we have."

Dustin didn't realize how drowsy he'd become. He rubbed his eyes and let the chatter of the birds in the high branches above him lull him to sleep. When he awakened, some time must have past. His father sat on a stump nearby, adjusting a hand tied fly onto the barb on the fly pole.

"Ready for some fishing?" Trent asked, a huge

grin on his face.

Dustin stood and stretched his aching muscles. "Yep," he answered, falling into step beside his father, with Tilly racing in front of them along the path.

***

Trent looked over at the horses on their walk to the lake. The mustangs stood quiet and content on the highline. This time of year the mosquitoes weren't too pesky, and the air was still too cold for flies, allowing for the horses to rest in peace.

A feeling of gratefulness at having his son here at his side warmed his heart. In these hills, he'd always found a peace that calmed him. The wilderness held a healing power along with a quiet solitude that tended to wash away one's woes. He hoped Dustin shared some of this contentment.

The poor kid had been through a lot the last few weeks. Trent couldn't remember his own mother, for she'd passed when he was younger than Dustin. But the void in his soul from her loss never went unnoticed. He couldn't imagine what that hole was like for his son.

"Dad—dad! I think I caught one."

Dustin pulled back on his pole, the tip of the rod bending forward.

"Bring him in, slow and easy. I'll pull him out for you when he gets close to the bank."

Trent kneeled at the water's edge, watching the plump trout zig and zag under the lake's glassy surface. Tilly barked with excitement beside him, snapping her jaws at the splashes.

"No girl, let me." Trent gently pushed the dog behind him.

Trent put his hands into the water, reaching for the fishing line. He pulled the trout toward him, until he could get his hands around its girth. In one fluid movement, he pulled the fish from the water and tossed it into the grass behind him.

"He's a fighter, that one." Trent chuckled. "That's one good looking fish, son. Great job."

The smile on Dustin's face proved priceless and would forever be ingrained in his memory.

CHAPTER NINE

They caught three fish in all, over the course of the afternoon. With each cast, Dustin waited in anticipation and wonderment for the telltale tug on the line as the trout bit at his fly. When they'd returned to camp, Trent showed him the proper way to clean and prepare their catch for cooking over the campfire.

"Let's let the fish bake while we take the horses to the meadow to graze. I'll show you how to hobble them."

Dustin led Scamp and Buck, while his dad ushered Gator and Arwin. The meadow grass grew lush from the spring rains and mountain streams.

"We'll hobble Buck first. You adjust the hobble between the hoof and the pastern on both front legs. I've worked with all these mustangs in advance, so they've learned not to fight it. It's always better to teach your horse something new at home before testing things out on the trail. It can be the difference between life and death out here."

Dustin nodded and started to hobble Scamp. Satisfied with how it looked, he gave the mustang a firm rub behind his ears, Scamp's favorite spot to have scratched. "Have some dinner, boy." Dustin wrapped his arms around his horse's neck and gave the gelding a hug.

"We'll come back after a bit. We'll let them fill their bellies awhile. When the sun starts to go down over the mountain, we'll walk back down and settle them on the highline for the night. It's time for us to fill our own bellies. Let's go eat some fish!"

The trout tasted better than anything Dustin had ever eaten before. He wasn't sure if it was his hunger or if the forest infused some magical element into one's food. After he finished, his eyelids drooped. The warmth of the fire made him drowsy, and he could hardly keep his eyes open.

"Why don't you head for your bedroll. You look plumb tuckered out. I'll go bring the horses in for the night by myself."

Dustin shook his head. "No, I'm coming to help." He stood and stretched his arms to the sky to work out the kinks in his shoulders and back before grabbing the horses' lead ropes from the stump where they had set them earlier. He started down the path, behind his father, Tilly at his heels.

"Your muscles will become accustomed to all this riding here in the next day or so. A person never realizes how many muscles they use to ride a horse until they've sat in the saddle a good eight-hour day." Trent let out a chuckle.

Dustin laughed, too. "Ya, I don't recall my backside hurting this bad from sitting at a desk all day at school."

Scamp raised his head and nickered, acknowledging their arrival.

"You take Scamp and Buck, I'll grab the other two," Trent directed.

"Time for bed, Scamp." Dustin snapped the lead rope to his horse's halter and unbuckled the hobbles. He led Scamp to where the other horse still grazed. Buck took several hopping steps away, but Dustin grabbed his halter before he could escape.

"Easy, boy." He took the hobbles off the mustang, and with Scamp and Buck in tow, started toward camp. The sun moved low behind the mountains, leaving the trail darkened and full of shadows. Yipping resonated in the distance and both horses let out a loud snort. Tilly remained close in front of him, but Buck danced around Scamp, pulling on the ropes.

"Sounds like coyotes. There are lots of them out here. Another good reason to highline the horses close to the campsite," Trent said.

A chill raced down Dustin's spine. He'd never heard coyotes before. In his mind, they were large wolf like dogs, fangs bared, growling and snapping.

"Will they bother us?"

"No, they shouldn't. They hunt at night. Yipping and howling lets the others know where they are and what they're doing. A type of communication they use."

Exhausted, Dustin put his concerns about the coyotes to the back of his mind. They settled the mustangs for the night and took a seat around the campfire a bit longer. Trent sipped on some coffee he'd set to brew while they were tending the horses. Dustin figured a cup of the hot beverage couldn't hurt. He plodded over to the pannier and found a cup in the pack, then headed to the fire, pulling the coffee pot from the coals.

"I probably shouldn't let you drink coffee," Trent mused, rubbing his jaw. "Guess it can't hurt, I started drinking it when I was about your age, maybe a smidgen younger, and it hasn't hurt me none."

Dustin nodded, taking a sip. The hot liquid warmed his insides. Though he wore a sweater, the breeze rustling through the trees gave him a chill. Tilly planted herself in front of his feet, resting her nose on his boot.

"Looks like you have your own personal foot warmer." Trent chuckled.

Dustin stroked the dog's head. "You can warm my feet any time you like, girl."

Unable to hold back a yawn or keep his eyes open a moment longer, he tossed the rest of the liquid into the bushes and placed his cup on a nearby stump.

"Night, dad."

"Good night, son. Get your rest."

Dustin made his way to the makeshift tent. He hunkered down in his sleeping bag and closed his eyes. The ground beneath him was hard and sloped downward, but he was too tired to care.

A loud clank woke him from a dead sleep. Dustin rose on his elbows and tried to focus outside the cover of the tarp. The coals from the fire still glowed, emitting some light, but not enough to see much of anything but dark shadows. A horse stomped its hoof in the distance. Another snorted. Tilly sat on her hunches at his side but didn't act worried.

Dustin waited and listened, but other than his father's rhythmic snoring, all was quiet.

He lay back and took a deep breath, trying to slow his heart-rate. *It must have been my imagination.* He closed his eyes and willed sleep to reclaim him.

The next time he opened his eyes, sunlight beat down on the cover, warming him through the plastic. Dustin rolled to his side. His dad still slept, cowboy hat positioned over his face to block out the light. He'd even used his saddle like a pillow. *Crazy.* Dustin loved Scamp, but to smell horse sweat and salty leather all night...

Dustin crawled out of his bag and yawned. The air still held a bite. He pulled his sweater down low on his back. Several coals still glowed in the fire-pit, so he gathered some small twigs and moss to cover them. A couple of lengthy blows and a flame ignited. He continued to feed the embers until a crackling fire emerged, emitting enough heat to warm his hands.

The horses nickered at him and stomped in place. "In a minute, guys," he called out. Feeling sorry for them, he walked over and scratched Scamp's neck. "Not much longer now, boy. When dad wakes up, we'll get you some breakfast."

Tilly followed him like a shadow as he gathered more firewood. He stacked the wood near the fire and grabbed the coffee pot. "Dad said the water's okay if it's boiled," he told the dog. Dustin started down the path to the lake to fill the pot.

Trent sat on a log next to the fire when he returned. "Looks like a scavenger got into our pack. Feasted on some of our nuts and jerky."

"I thought I heard a noise during the night. I should've woke you. Tilly didn't seem worried, so I fell back asleep."

"No worries. Tonight we'll make sure to put our food away so the critters can't steal it." Trent smiled. "Happens sometimes. I know better and should've checked before I crashed in my bedroll."

They finished out the morning sitting around the campfire eating a quick breakfast of oatmeal and coffee. When breakfast was done, they walked the horses to the lake for a drink.

"We'll let the horses graze an hour or so, then we'll get moving. Help me get them hobbled."

While the mustangs foraged for their morning meal, Dustin whittled on a piece of wood with his pocket knife while Trent tossed a stick for Tilly to fetch.

"It's so quiet out here, how can you stand to do this on your own?" Dustin asked. His father must get lonely, with no one to talk to except his horses and the dog.

"I love it. It's not quiet at all if you think about it. Stop and listen, there's a million noises right now. I never enjoyed big crowds or city life. My horse and wide-open places are what make me truly happy. Other than my whirlwind relationship with your mother, I've always been this way. A loner, more at home with my horse and dog than with most folks I know."

Dustin grew quiet and fidgeted with the string on his hoodie. His mind flooded with unanswered questions and doubts. Does my dad really want me here with him then? Will my being here take away from his happiness? Will he send me back to grandma and grandpa after a while? He stood and walked away, using a tree to block his dad from seeing the worry erupting from him.

"Hey, let's get the horses ready and start the day," Trent called out, tossing the last of his coffee into the bushes.

Trent walked toward the grazing horses. Dustin lagged behind, fighting tears and fiddling with Scamp's lead rope to regain his composure instead of helping. His father's words for some reason had crushed him.

"What's wrong, son? Let's start leading the horses to camp."

Dustin grabbed Buck's lead rope from Trent and led the horses away. Maybe I should do my dad a favor and ask to go back to California. He recalled his grandparent's warning before his departure. "Your father is nothing but a recluse," his grandmother had said with disdain thick in her voice. Now, Dustin worried if he was a hindrance to his father.

Dustin's heart dropped to his stomach. He was an outcast here on this ranch. His father's life-style was meant for one. He'd said this is how he liked it. Why wouldn't he have fought his mom to see him all these years past if not? Trent liked being alone. Hurt surged through Dustin's veins and his throat grew tight with this knowledge.

He slogged through the rest of the morning. What little conversation he shared with his father was stilted, at least on Dustin's side. All he could think was what a burden he must be for his father. Every so often, Dustin caught his father casting a glance at him, a questioning look on his face. He never offered to discuss anything with him though. Dustin came to the conclusion he didn't want to.

The next several days were long and drawn out for Dustin as guilt and worry plagued him. Still he didn't speak to his dad, even when his father asked several times what was bothering him. Scamp must have sensed his heartache. The happy-go-lucky mustang became moody and irritable, pinning his ears back at the other mustangs and swishing his tail, when the other horses came too close.

Tilly whined and ran back and forth between Dustin and Trent. She could sense the distress in him. By the fifth day, the whole camp was up in arms.

"Dustin, it's time we had a talk. Something's eating away at you. I can see it in your eyes. You refuse to speak more than several words at a time to me. What's going on?" Trent's voice was laced with concern.

Dustin's heart pounded, and his palms started to dampen. How could the guy not know? Distracted, he kicked at a rock. The pebble flew into the air and hit Tilly on her side, causing her to let out a loud yelp.

"Now that's enough," Trent's voice held an edge of frustration. "Talk to me now, son. What's wrong?"

Dustin's head ached. Tears burned in his eyes. He hadn't meant for the rock to hit Tilly. Now his father stood before him staring hard, demanding an answer he didn't have.

"Nothing's wrong. Please, just leave me alone." His heart pounded like a clawhammer against his ribs with those painful words. When he looked into his dad's face, he saw nothing but sadness. Unable to stand it a moment longer, he did the only thing he could. He walked away.

***

Trent scratched his head in confusion. Where had he gone wrong? He thought he'd found a real connection with Dustin with this camping trip. Thought this excursion would help them grow closer. He was giving his son insight to the life he enjoyed living.

The last few days he'd seen the torment in Dustin's eyes. Only, he didn't know how to reach out to the boy. To show him how much he cared. How much he loved having him here with him. Words to express this feeling evaded him. He'd never been one big on words and now it was proving to be his downfall.

The boy will come around. Just give him some time and space. Trent cared for the horses and set camp for the night. He couldn't see Dustin but knew Tilly would remain at his side. The dog would guard him with her life. She'd loved Dustin from the moment he set foot on the ranch. Dogs like Tilly were loyal to a fault, and she proved herself one of the best.

Trent listened to the zipper on Dustin's sleeping bag open. Tilly came over and sniffed his face, as if letting him know the boy was safe. With his son near, his heartbeat slowed, and he let himself start to drift off. Tomorrow would be a new day. A day for reconciliation.

CHAPTER TEN

The next two days were painfully silent. Dustin kept his eyes downcast and rode behind the pack horses to avoid his dad. He tried to harden his heart against what was sure to come. He knew his father would send him packing when they returned to the ranch. Why wouldn't he, after the way Dustin had treated him?

The worst part would be leaving Scamp behind. He'd always admired horses and couldn't ask for one better than the little bay mustang. They'd forged a solid bond over the last couple of weeks. Dustin would miss his quiet strength, and silly horse antics that made him laugh, like when Scamp searched his coat looking for a treat. Or, the soft horse muzzle caressing his cheek.

Dustin swiped at an escaped tear and focused on the path. They traveled single file along the side of the mountain, a dizzying ravine on their outside leg. He'd never feared heights but staring down into the rocky abyss sent a shudder down his spine.

So far, on this trip, they'd braved narrow wooden bridges to cross fast moving creeks, climbed steep hillsides, and navigated a raging river with water reaching clear to Scamp's chest. They'd even rode through a boggy meadow, where the horses' hooves made a sucking pop with each step, making him chuckle.

The mustangs did not appreciate this at all, and he'd sighed in relief after making it safely across the bog without any mishaps. Dustin wondered if they'd see any snow. His dad had mentioned they may come across some at the higher elevations, but up till now there had been none.

By noon, the group reached a pasture full of wildflowers of every color imaginable. Burnt reds, sunny yellows, mixed into a field of various shades of green grasses. The picture before him was something his mother would have loved.

His shoulders drooped, and his chin trembled with the sudden thought of her. Sorrow clung to him like a festering wound. A scab would form, then a memory would tear it away and reopen his mind to the pain.

A well-worn path wound through the meadow. Dustin glanced ahead and noticed the packhorse, Gator, suddenly pin his ears back. The mustang's tail tucked under his hind legs. The horse let out a grunt and started bucking and snorting. Arwin copied the gelding's actions, arching her back with hooves flying through the air like razors.

Trent dropped their lead. "Dustin, get out of here!" he yelled, his voice laced with alarm.

Terror gripped him like a vise as the scene unfolded before his eyes. Scamp froze in place, his ears pinned flat. A sharp needle-like sting on his neck snapped him to attention. He swatted at his face. A loud buzzing noise vibrated against his ear, and it dawned on him what was happening.

"Ha!" he shrieked and kicked at Scamp's sides. The horse turned on his haunches and bolted. Dustin grabbed for the saddle horn and leaned low against the mustang's mane. His face and neck burned as the assault continued. They ran and ran, until Scamp's shoulders were covered in a foamy lather, and Dustin wondered if he could hold on another minute.

He pulled Scamp to a halt and jumped off. His fingers burned, the skin angry and red started to welt from the assault. He bent over, gasping for each breath. Scamp snorted and pawed the ground next to him, trembling. "Easy boy. It's going to be okay," he said aloud, to calm the horse and himself. Dustin rested his hands on his knees and looked up, then over his shoulder.

Where's dad? He should've followed. Tilly had trailed him, so his dad wouldn't have her to show him where he and Scamp were. The poor dog lay panting at his feet, exhausted and traumatized as the rest of them.

Fear ripped through him once more. He sat in the dirt and propped his head in his hands. With every heartbeat, his head throbbed against his palms. Tired. He felt so tired; closing his eyes, he rested his back on the ground.

He counted each breath while he waited for his dad to appear. Trent would come. It would be easier for his dad to find him if he stayed put. They'd discussed this plan if there was an emergency.

Trent never showed. Dustin squinted into the horizon, unsure how much time might have past. The sun now hung low behind the mountains and the air felt cooler than before. Though he was chilled, his skin burned where the bees had repeatedly stung him on the hands, face and neck, leaving behind puffy, tender bumps.

Dustin walked over to check Scamp. Small hard bumps appeared over the horse's neck and rump. He stroked the mustang's shoulder, contemplating what he should do. They'd made an emergency plan and it required Dustin would remain in place until his dad could find him. Too much time had passed though. Uneasy, he paced to and fro. The only explanation was his dad must be in trouble.

"Let's go, Scamp. Tilly, let's head out. We need to find out what happened to dad." Dustin adjusted the cinch on the mustang's saddle and pulled his weary body onto the horse's back. The small group back-tracked along the trail. He was unsure how far they had traveled. He didn't think they'd gone too far, but none of the scenery looked familiar.

They walked through a strand of timbers. A large meadow loomed in the horizon. Now he recalled the spot. He remembered thinking how his mother would have loved those flowers in the field they'd entered, before everything fell apart.

"Tilly, find dad," he ordered, while nudging Scamp with his heels. Tilly scurried off, nose to the dirt, as he and Scamp trailed behind.

"Dustin! Over here," Trent's voice echoed in the distance.

Tilly barked with urgency.

Dustin searched the grass. Where is he? Off to the left, he caught sight of a hand waving above the colorful wildflowers.

"Dad!" He hopped off Scamp and ran. He found his father crumpled on the ground.

"Boy, I'm sure glad to see you. It's been one heck of a long day." The relief in his dad's voice made Dustin cringe. *If I'd only come sooner.*

He hardly recognized his father. Trent's face was covered in welts and perspiration. Tilly licked his cheek, still barking with joy.

"Are you okay?" Dustin asked, unable to keep a steady voice. "I'm sorry it took so long for me to get back here." Panic clinched his guts. Realization of how dangerous a predicament they were in was setting in.

"Dustin, listen close. I'm in a bad way. I hate to do this to you, but there's no getting around it. I need you to hop back on Scamp and head down the trail. Find us some help. I broke my leg when I fell. I'm not able to move."

"What! I can't leave you. What if I get lost? We said we'd stay together, no matter what," his voice cracked. Terrible images of his dad dying flashed in his mind. His stomach knotted, the shock of it doubling him over. He couldn't leave his dad like this.

The temperature continued to drop, and a brisk wind had picked up speed as dusk closed in on them. Dustin shivered from both fear and the cold.

"You have to, son. I'm losing blood and growing weaker by the moment. The mustangs all scattered when those hornets attacked. I wouldn't be able to ride Buck even if he hadn't run off. There is no other choice. You have to leave now. Scamp will take care of you. Put your trust in him and let him take you back to the ranch."

Tears burned in the back of Dustin's eyes, and he crumpled to his knees.

"Please don't make me go. I'm scared." His body trembled with the admission.

"I know you are, son. But I need you to do this for me. You're tough. This is the last thing I ever thought I'd ask of you, but I'm in real trouble here."

Dustin peered at his father's leg. It was bent at an odd angle and the denim was crimson with the man's blood. He swallowed hard.

"Tonight will be cold," his voice shook with the words.

"Do a quick search of the perimeter. See if anything fell off the horses when they spooked," Trent instructed, his voice hoarse.

Dustin stood and quickly did his father's bidding. He explored the meadow. He couldn't find anything in the looming darkness and time was wasting.

"Sorry, Dad. Nothing."

When he glanced down, he noticed his dad's

face was pale under all the bumps, and slick with sweat, even in the fading light.

"If you ride out now, hard and fast, but safe, mind you, maybe you'll run into someone on the trail who can help. If not, at a fast clip you should reach the ranch in two days at most."

Two days. It sounded like a lifetime to Dustin. He walked over and collected Scamp's reins. He racked his brain for a better answer. Maybe he could fasten some kind of bed for Scamp to pull behind him. These ideas would all take time. Something they were short on. The only thing left was to ride hard and fast for the ranch through the night and pray someone else would be on the trail who could signal for help.

Dustin searched his saddlebags; finding some matches, an idea sparked.

"Dad, I'm going to build you a fire before I go. The temperature's dropping, and I don't want you to freeze to death before I return. I'll set wood close by, so you can toss it in without moving around too much."

He didn't wait for an answer. He scooped twigs and pieces of wood into his arms until he couldn't see over his load and carried them to his father. He lit a small fire, placing stones around the perimeter to prevent the dry grasses from burning. Happy with the result, he felt a little better about parting from his father to find help.

"Thanks, son. This was a great idea."

"I'm leaving you with my canteen and the

extra snacks from my pack. It will help to keep up your strength."

Dustin set several protein bars and a bag of jerky beside his father.

"Take one for yourself. You'll need it," Trent said, his words barely reaching a whisper.

"I'll be back quick as I can." Dustin quickly turned his head away from Trent's wounded form. He stroked Tilly's head.

"You stay here with dad, girl. I'll be back soon."

Dustin hoisted himself into the saddle.

"I know you will, son. Please...be careful out there. Don't take any unnecessary risks. Let that mustang take care of you, and don't worry about me. I'll be fine."

A bolt of dread settled into his stomach. What if things turned for the worse? What if he never saw his father alive again? Panic gripped him like a vise, he couldn't concentrate. Thoughts of horror filled his mind.

"I'm sorry for the way I acted these last few days. I didn't mean any of it." The words spilled out and he couldn't stop the tears from running down his cheeks. He was leaving his dad to die, he just knew it. He couldn't bear to lose him.

"I know you didn't. You're a fine boy. You've made me proud these last few weeks. I should have told you sooner, but I've never been good with sharing my feelings out loud. I couldn't have asked for a better son. Now go, please. And remember, Scamp will take care of you, if you let him have his head."

***

Trent fought to keep the panic from his voice. He watched his son's features ease up with his words. He wished he could say more, but as it was, he fought to keep consciousness. If he failed and succumbed to the darkness, Dustin might not leave him and bring the help he desperately needed.

CHAPTER ELEVEN

Dustin turned Scamp in a circle, nudging him with his heels into a run down the trail. Though the path through the trees was dark, the mustang continued to move in a steady, ground-eating gallop. They kept this pace for what seemed an eternity. Dustin lay low over Scamp's neck, the horse's mane whipping against his cheeks. The insides of his legs had rubbed raw hours ago and ached from the grip he held to keep himself upright in the saddle.

They soon reached a river. He dreaded crossing this in the dark of night. The water roared, making it all the more ominous. He pulled Scamp to a halt and stepped out of the saddle. On wobbly legs he rested his shoulder against the mustang's side. His legs were like tree stumps attached to his hips, but he managed to lead the horse to the water's edge. Scamp drank his fill and tossed his muzzle in the air, sprinkling water over Dustin.

Though his mouth felt full of cotton balls, he refrained from drinking from the river. He'd left his canteen with his dad, along with the water tablets. If he drank, it could possibly make him deathly ill. He didn't have time to be sick. Instead, he splashed his face and moistened his lips before standing.

A sliver of a moon in the vast black sky cast enough light to reflect off the river. His pulse raced as he watched the water rush in swirling eddies downstream. He took a deep breath, conjuring the courage to make this crossing.

Every muscle in his body screamed with retaliation when he pulled himself into the saddle. The air was crisp, and he shivered, but he ignored the goosebumps rising on his arms. If he felt cold, his dad must be freezing.

"Go!" Scamp leaped forward, then paused at the edge of the bank. *Let Scamp do the work*, his father had said. He lowered the reins, giving the horse his head. The mustang took his first step into the rushing water and hesitated. Scamp's ears shot forward and he snorted. When nothing happened, the gelding took another step. Then another. Dustin held tight to the saddle horn while Scamp made his way across. The water reached the bottoms of his boots this time, but they were better than halfway across.

"Good boy...good boy," Dustin cooed and patted the horse's neck. Scamp finished the last few feet with ease and jumped onto the bank. Once on firm footing, the horse shook the water off like a dog, shaking him in the saddle like the spin cycle on a washing machine.

Dustin took hold of the reins. Scamp tossed his head. "What's wrong?" He hopped off and looked the mustang over. The bridle hung loose, the bit low in the gelding's mouth. He reached for the headstall and noticed the cheek piece had severed and come apart. The bridle was now useless.

Dustin removed the bit from Scamp's mouth and tossed the headstall to the ground. The horse still had a halter on. He took the lead rope and fastened it over Scamp's neck, attaching it to the loop on the other side. It would have to do.

Before remounting, Dustin did a quick check of his saddle, adjusting the cinch. Satisfied Scamp was comfortable, he mounted and cued the horse into a gallop once more. They ran through the night at a steady clip, stopping every so often to rest and catch their breath.

The forest and its dark shadows were the worst. When they passed through a cover of trees, coyotes howled in the distance. Dustin bit back his fear and Scamp increased his pace without any urging. They rode through meadows, climbed hills, slid down ravines, all in the cloak of darkness.

When the sun rose the next morning, they stopped along the edge of a rocky bluff. Dustin scanned the horizon. A hawk floated in the air, searching for prey, no doubt, he thought. None of the landscape before him looked familiar. What if we're going the wrong direction? We may never find help and dad will die. The thought made him shudder.

Trust in Scamp, he'll take you home. His father's words kept him sane. He stroked the horse's neck and pressed his heels into the gelding's sides. "I trust you boy. Take me home." Scamp moved out at a ground eating trot, ears forward toward his destination.

The day wore on. Still no signs of anyone else on the trail. Dustin's stomach rolled and clinched with hunger. His lips, now parched and cracked, stuck together like glue. There was no spit left to swallow inside his mouth.

Dustin noticed a darkness lingering in the distance. Sinister clouds drew closer with each mile. The air changed from cool one moment, to balmy the next. Gusts of wind blew Scamp's mane into his face, along with dust and dirt from the trail. The mustang's ears moved forward and back, like twin beacons, and he snorted and crow-hopped every few steps. The hair on Dustin's arms stood on end. He could no longer hear the birds singing their daytime melodies.

In the far distance, a flash of light caught his attention. A loud cracking boom shook the ground beneath them moments later, sending Scamp skittering sideways. Dustin grabbed the horn to keep himself in the saddle. He pulled the horse to a stop.

The storm rushed at them like a frenzied beast. Unsure of what to do, he stayed put and watched nature's wrath explode around them. With the thunder and lightning came hail. Small BB sized pellets peppered them both. His face and neck stung from the assault. He urged the mustang into a run for the trees.

Scamp reared, then crow hopped. Dustin squeezed his eyes shut and clung to the saddle horn. He let out a sigh of relief when they reached the low laying branches protecting them from the tiny balls of fury bombarding the earth.

The storm passed quickly, giving them a breather. In its place, a fine, misty rain followed, bringing with it a bone-tingling chill. Again, thoughts of his dad and how he fared in this weather spurred Dustin forward. They moved on at a slow jog. It was more comfortable than a full on run, and easier for Scamp to maintain for longer periods of time.

Dustin's head bobbed up and down with each hoofbeat. His eyeballs were gritty and sore and when he shut them, a warm peace washed over him, luring him into the soothing darkness. It wasn't until he noticed a change in Scamp's gait, that his eyes flew open. He blinked several times, adjusting to the sun overhead. It's rays bright against the freshly watered earth.

Scamp slid on his hocks down the side of a mountain and down sharp switchbacks only a sure-footed mustang could maneuver. Below, a movement caught Dustin's attention. Was that a person? He raised his hand above his eyes to block the sun and squinted, trying to see if there was someone there or if he was wishful thinking.

A blue shirt swayed in and out of the trees like a ghost. His imagination went into overdrive. *A real person?* "Hello!" Dustin yelled, raising out of the saddle. His throat was too parched, and the word came out crackled. He tried again, but lost track of the vision. Scamp didn't seem curious or worried like he would if someone or something was near.

"Hello?" he called out again. He urged Scamp to move faster down the hillside, swallowing his fear as they started to slide. When they reached the flats, Dustin brought the mustang to a halt and hollered some more. There were no return calls. His heart dropped. He'd hoped help would be waiting at the bottom. Discouraged and near tears, he spurred the gelding forward. Dustin scanned the trail looking for signs of hoof prints. There were none.

More time passed when they reached a small stream. The first water they'd come across since the treacherous river crossing of the night before. Dustin lowered himself to the ground, falling to his knees. His body weak from lack of food and dehydration, he crawled toward the water. Unable to withstand his thirst any longer, he drank beside Scamp at the stream. Never had water tasted so sweet.

The water revived him somewhat. He lay in the tall grass along the bank and let Scamp rest. The horse nibbled at the lush grasses next to the creek as Dustin closed his eyes and let the warmth of the late afternoon sun warm his tired body.

With great weariness, he mustered the last of his ebbing strength and forced himself to stand. To trudge on. His dad needed his help, and he didn't know where he was or how far they'd come. All he knew was his bottom was chapped and saddle sore and he still had a ways to travel.

Dustin pulled himself back into the saddle.

He clucked his tongue and Scamp stepped out. Dustin scanned the area for signs of a blue jacket, but nothing moved in the forest, other than the birds, which flew from tree to tree when they rode by. No person emerged from the timbers. His imagination had played cruel tricks on him, he realized, as a hard knot of despair lodged in his throat.

When dusk settled in, bringing forth the shadows of the night, Dustin suspected he'd rode well over twenty-four hours at this point. Surely, he'd find someone to help him? He continued on, occasionally nodding off, letting sleep ease the fears continuing to plague his mind.

The moon cast a shimmery light across the wild landscape. He'd made it off the mountain and into more open terrain. Sloping meadows and valleys, instead of the steep cliffs and mountains.

Dustin kept his hands tucked into his armpits and chin nestled against his chest to retain his body heat. He closed his eyes and let his mind wander to a safe place, where peril didn't lurk at every turn. He thought it a great plan until Scamp froze in his tracks and started to snort and blow, pawing at the earth with his front hoof. This could only mean one thing. Danger was ahead.

***

Trent opened his eyes. Darkness had settled for the night, and the cool mountain air chilled him to the bone. He tried to inch closer to the fire Dustin had built him and tossed a couple sticks on the flames.

"Here Tilly girl," he called. The dog rose from her vantage point and lay at his side, resting her muzzle against his chest, staring at him with anxious brown eyes.

He rubbed her soft fur. "Let's pray Dustin is safe. And finds help soon." He worried for his son. Scamp might be one heck of a mustang but being in charge of carrying a green horn and a child to boot down a mountain for help was a lot to ask.

Trent had survived lots of scrapes and couldn't count the times he'd been tossed from a horse in his ranching/rodeo career. But never had he been in a position where he was accountable for someone else. His son.

He should've never taken Dustin into these mountains. The boy had never stepped off the pavement until he'd met Trent. To whisk him straight into the wilderness and make him responsible for finding help on his own. A green boy, a wild mustang, and nothing but miles and miles of wild blue yonder all around them. What in the world had he been thinking?

Frustration and pain pummeled him in equal quantities. "There's nothing I can do about it now, is there Tilly girl?" He took a deep breath to quiet his nerves and caressed the dog's warm fur. Tilly moved closer and lay stretched out beside him, her back to his hip, sharing her warmth.

Trent shut his eyes. Sleep evaded him. He tried to shift his weight, but the discomfort from the movement racked his body, and he gasped for each breath. Once the agonizing pain stilled, he attempted to calm his thoughts by staring into the stars. One by one he counted, anything to keep his mind off Dustin's fate on the mountain.

CHAPTER TWELVE

The hair on Dustin's arms stood on end. "Easy boy. Easy," he cooed to calm Scamp. The smell of wood smoke, faint as a whisper on the breeze, caught his attention. Where there's fire, there must be humans! His heart hammered against his ribs. *Hang in there dad, help will be on the way!*

The wind blew toward them, so the campers were somewhere ahead, he hoped. Dustin urged Scamp into a gallop. "Help, help," he yelled at the top of his lungs. There was no answer to his calls, but from the time of night, the folks would most likely be sleeping, he reasoned.

The scent of smoke continued to grow stronger with each stride Scamp took. Dustin scanned both sides of the trail, searching for a clue to where the campers might be. *I'll never find them.* He refused to let despair defeat him.

"Steady, boy." He stroked the horse's neck. Scamp picked up speed, ears straight ahead. "Hello? Is someone there? Please let there be someone." Dustin's breaths became short and fast as he looked around.

Off to the left, in the distance, two horses stood highlined. Flames from a fire could be seen behind them with a tent on the far side. *People!* Dustin sighed with relief. He kicked Scamp's sides and the horse bolted forward.

The tied horses stood alert and watched their approach.

"Who's there?" A man's gruff voice called from inside the tent.

"Help!" he yelled, pulling Scamp to a halt by the fire so he could see his surroundings.

"I need help, sir. My dad's hurt."

Dustin heard the creak of a zipper, then a man stepped out of the shelter, pulling on a denim jacket. "How far up the trail is he, son?"

"I'm not sure. I've been riding fast and steady since yesterday afternoon."

"Go ahead and get down from your horse. I'll make you some hot chocolate to warm you so you can give me the details."

"Steve, what's going on?" A woman, tall and slender, with braided gray hair that hung to her waist, stepped out of the tent. "What's happened?"

"Carla, this boy says his dad's on up the mountain, and injured. Let's get him and his horse settled, and I'll head back down the road and send a call out for some assistance."

The man named Steve handed him a cup of steaming coco.

"Thank you." Dustin cradled the warm brew between his hands, soaking in the heat.

Steve stood by the fire. The man's red beard glowed against the flames. "You feel ready to tell us your story, so I can let the authorities know as much as possible when I call them?"

Dustin nodded and looked into the man's deep green eyes. "My dad and I have been out here about a week. We had two horses and two pack animals with us. Yesterday, we were riding through a meadow and were attacked by bees. My horse, Scamp, spooked and ran off with me on his back.

"When I was able to get him stopped, we waited for my dad to find us. I waited too long. He never showed. Scamp and I had to return to the meadow. I found him on the ground and all the other horses gone. His leg didn't look right and there was a lot of blood." He shuddered with the memory. " He told me to go for help. I left him with a fire and all the supplies from my saddlebags. Our dog, Tilly, is with him, too."

"Sounds like a grand adventure gone wrong. We'll find your dad; don't you worry none. We'll get him the help he needs. I'm going to ride down the trail until I can get a signal on my phone to call for help." Steve handed his cup to Carla.

"Please have them call my dad's boss. Dad discussed where we'd be with them. Mr. and Mrs. Smith of the Old Bay Mare Ranch. They may be able to give you better directions of where we were on the hill."

"I've heard good things about that ranch. I'll be sure to get word to them," Steve said.

"Get some rest. I'm going to go take care of your horse and see Steve off." A warm hand clasped his shoulder. Carla's kind smile was reassuring.

The couple walked away from the fire. Carla grabbed Scamp's lead rope.

"Where's your bridle?" she paused, her voice curious as she looked at him over her shoulder.

"It fell off a while back," he answered.

"This is a nice little horse you have here." Carla ran her hand down Scamp's neck.

"He's the best. A mustang from the Ochoco herd," his voice burst with pride.

"They are some fine mustangs," Carla agreed. "Steve and I come across a wild herd of them out here sometimes. Beautiful horses."

Dustin watched the couple move about the camp from his seat by the warmth of the fire. Steve saddled his horse and quickly disappeared into the darkness. Carla settled Scamp in next to the remaining animal and started back toward the campfire. She stopped by her tent for a moment and disappeared inside. A second later, she came out with a blanket in hand.

"Here, wrap yourself in this and try and get some shut eye. Soon as daylight hits, things will be busy around here."

She didn't have to ask twice. Dustin closed his eyes and drifted into oblivion. Only, with sleep came dreams. Not peaceful dreams, but unsettling images of his dad writhing in pain. In his dream, his father convulsed from the cold, the fire down to coals with no remaining wood within reach.

Dustin woke with a gasp. Carla, who sat on the opposite side of the campfire from him, glanced over.

"You okay?"

"Sure, just a bad dream." He wrapped the blanket tighter around his shoulders.

Dustin willed himself to stay awake from then on. He stood and paced by the fire. He checked on Scamp, giving the horse a good rub behind the ears.

"I'm back!" Steve trotted back into camp and dismounted.

"Help will be on the way at first light. We'll get the fire blazing, so the Sheriff and Search and Rescue crew can find us. And Dustin, the Smiths are on their way. Bill's sure a nice fellow. He and Betty are going to haul a couple horses to the east trailhead and ride in. They were going to leave soon as we got off the phone, so I expect they'll make it here around daybreak, same as the rescue crew coming in by ATV."

Anxiety simmered into a full boil in Dustin's gut. How much longer until daylight? he wondered, walking to and fro until a well worn-path was ground into the dirt. He did this for hours, refusing to sit when Carla asked him to. As if an answer to his question, the sun rose from behind the tree line, bringing with it the chatter of early birds as they searched for their breakfast.

"Dustin?"

The sound of Betty's voice in the distance was a welcome relief.

Dustin ran to Betty. She and Bill stood beside their saddled horses. He dove into Betty's arms, finding the solace he needed there. She stroked his hair and patted his back as the tears poured down his cheeks.

"It's okay. We'll find him and he'll be fine. Your dad's a strong man," she told him, a look of conviction on her weathered face.

While Betty calmed him, Bill walked ahead and stood with his horse next to the fire, shaking Steve and Carla's hands. Now that Betty and Bill were near, he felt safe. Everything would be all right.

Minutes later, the sounds of ATVs and human voices could be heard. The Search and Rescue crew had arrived. Betty stood aside with him, while the group gathered and discussed travel plans for the area. Dustin had told Bill all he could remember about the journey down the mountain. Most of the way he'd stuck to trails that appeared well-traveled, but Scamp had chosen the route and it was dark for a lot of the ride.

"Let's go," a man yelled from the seat of his red four-wheeler. He pulled his baseball cap low and started the engine. Beside and behind him, others did the same. Bill and Steve stood by their saddled horses.

"Dustin, would you rather wait here until they find your dad?" Betty asked.

"No, I'm going back up there. I need to make sure he's okay."

Betty rubbed his shoulder. "I understand. I'd do the same. Let's get going, we've a long ride in front of us."

The group rode at a ground eating trot. The ATVs echoed in the distance, well ahead of them. Every so often, the small group stopped to let the horses rest. Though tired, the urgency to find his dad alive and well kept him alert. Scamp was in much better condition, rested and ready to go even after his journey of carrying Dustin off the mountain.

A mustang, he was bred for this kind of travel. Bill and Betty's mounts, also mustangs, had no problem keeping pace behind the four-wheelers. Steve and Carla made more frequent stops on their horses, not being conditioned for this speed on the terrain they crossed.

When nightfall fell over the mountains, the group stopped to refuel horses, engines, and themselves.

"We're not going to stop for the night, are we?" A wave of panic ran through Dustin with the thought. His dad couldn't survive much longer with his injury, could he? And being alone another night in the cold? Dustin shivered at the thought.

Betty took him aside. "Dustin, the four-wheelers are going to call it a day and rest, then get an early start in the morning at first light. It's not safe for them to traverse these mountain slopes in the dark."

"No! They can't quit now," he cried, his voice shrill with alarm.

"Dustin, listen. Bill and I, and the sheriff, are

going to continue the search. Bill has a first aid kit if we are able to find Trent first. You can come with us if you feel you can keep up the pace."

"I'm coming with you."

"I knew you would." She patted his back. "Get something to eat. We'll be heading out again here shortly."

Dustin grabbed a plate of beans and cornbread from one of the volunteers at the makeshift cook station. "Thanks," he remembered his manners and stepped to the side so others could get their food. He sucked down the meal along with a soda. Refreshed, he trotted over to Bill.

"Ready, son?"

"Let's find my dad."

With a nod, Bill tipped his hat and started for his horse.

***

Trent moved in and out of consciousness. Though cold, his body felt numb, his limbs dead weight. He'd run out of firewood hours ago. His thoughts wandered to Dustin. Had he made it down the mountain? Had he and Scamp encountered any danger? His mind raced with worry for his son. He knew of the dangers which lurked in the wilderness.

A flood of guilt washed over him. Poor Dustin. They'd just found each other, and now Trent would be leaving him, too. The boy would be an orphan, alone in the world. There were the grandparents. But Dustin didn't speak none to fondly of them. Maybe Bill and Betty could raise him? All these thoughts fatigued him more.

A coyote howled nearby. Tilly, still by his side, let out a whimper and a yip. "It's okay, girl," he tried to sooth her, his voice hoarse from lack of moisture. The dog seemed anxious, but he didn't have the strength to console her further. He needed to maintain what little energy he had left to survive.

CHAPTER THIRTEEN

The tall Ponderosa's swayed, their limbs moaning in the wind. The trail seemed less frightening when riding with others. Dustin straightened his shoulders and followed behind Bill and Betty, heart full of courage. Bill had a headlamp attached to his hat, lighting the path before them.

When they came to the river crossing, Dustin was comforted in the fact he remembered this, and they were on the right track.

A new energy surged through his veins. They were closer to locating his dad.

"I can't believe you rode through this river by yourself, Dustin. I bet you were terrified. You are your father's son, brave and strong," Betty remarked, her words choked.

"Thanks," he said, his voice small and meek. His focus remained on moving forward. On finding his father.

At daybreak, they stopped to rest the animals and discuss their course, while wolfing down a cheese bagel and drinking coffee from a thermos Betty had brought along.

"I've ridden along this trail in the past. Tell me again, everything you can recall about where you left your father," Bill urged.

Dustin closed his eyes, trying to bring forth images of the surrounding area where his dad lay waiting.

"I can't remember anything else." He squeezed his eyes tighter, trying to recollect something, anything which might be of help.

"Wait! I do remember a small meadow, smaller than the others, full of grass and lots of flowers." He struggled to remember any detail to separate it from all the other blossom filled meadows they'd passed through. *The rock.* He remembered a large boulder with claw marks running down the length of it, like long cat scratches.

"There was a rock with jagged marks down the side when I went collecting wood for dad's fire. It lay at the bottom of the hill, like it had slid down and stopped before rolling into the grass."

"Bingo, son. That's exactly what I needed. I think I know precisely where you're talking about. And the good news is, it's not far from here! I know a shortcut up this mountain which will get us there faster."

The group mounted and rode forward with renewed spirits. They left ribbons tied to tree branches to let the others know the direction they'd taken. The mountain was steep with loose soil and rocks that skittered back down as the horse's struggled to make their way toward the top.

They had to dismount near the peak and lead the animals the last few yards. Dustin put his trust in Scamp and let the horse pick his footing. When they reached safety, Bill turned and gave them a wide grin. "Aren't you glad we have mustangs?"

Betty tilted her head to the right. "I can smell a tinge of wood smoke in the wind. We must be close."

"The meadow we're looking for shouldn't be far ahead," Dustin yelled out, urging Scamp forward.

The group increased their speed. The sound of engines grew louder behind them. The ATVs would be there soon. They galloped through a cluster of trees and into a grassy meadow.

"This is the place!" Dustin pulled Scamp to a halt. Bill and Betty did the same. He stood in his stirrups and glanced around the area. His dad should be here somewhere.

"Dad?" he hollered. "Dad!"

Only a blue jay in the distance answered his call. Hopes dashed, Dustin fought the tears threatening to escape.

"Don't worry, son. We'll find him," Bill said, trying to sound reassuring.

But Dustin caught Bill's worried expression as he tilted his head toward Betty. He glanced away and into the tree line. This was where he'd left his dad, it had to be.

"Let's ride ahead, see if that rock's up farther." Bill nudged his horse and moved out.

"Hey, wait. I think I heard something." Dustin's heart pounded as he froze in place.

They all paused. Dustin held his breath, willing the noise to happen again.

Ruff, ruff.

"Tilly!" He urged Scamp into a gallop. "Tilly, come here, girl."

The dog rushed forward, head low, tail tucked between her back legs.

"What's wrong? Oh no." Dustin jumped off Scamp and ran the direction Tilly had emerged from.

"He's here. Bill, over here," he cried frantically.

Dustin ran and fell to his knees beside his father's form.

Trent lay shivering, perspiration dotting his forehead. His skin was white as chalk. The red welts from the bee stings had festered and oozed, creating yellow crust covered scabs over his face and arms.

"Dad, can you hear me? I found help." He reached for his father's hand and gave it a squeeze. This brought a smile to the man's lips, then a grimace.

"Trent. It's Bill here, help is on the way. We're going to get you patched up. You're going to be just fine."

Dustin stood to the side while Betty and Bill worked over his dad.

"Dustin, I can hear the four-wheelers coming. Start waving your arms when you see them to direct them over here."

He did as he was told, not sure what else he could do. Behind him, Betty spoke on the two-way radio, describing his dad's condition to someone on the other end before saying thank you and over and out.

"Don't fret none." She walked over and placed a warm hand on his shoulder. They've kept a helicopter on standby. They're sending it over now. There's plenty of room here for them to land and pick up your dad."

Dustin nodded. Exhaustion was taking a toll on him and he struggled to remain standing.

"Why don't you have a seat, Dustin? You look like you've been hit by a raging bull, twice over."

The suggestion sounded good. He couldn't recall ever being so tired. He sank to the ground. Tilly quickly curled herself into his lap, licking his hand. He rested his head against hers, closing his eyes and letting his mind drift.

"Betty...come here, quick."

The words ripped through his system like a jagged knife. He opened his eyes to see Betty dash to her husband's side. What more could possibly go wrong?

CHAPTER FOURTEEN

Dustin remained by his dad's side, clutching the gurney as the medic helped load him into the helicopter. Only he and Betty would be allowed in the chopper for the flight to the hospital. The nurse worked over his father, adjusting the tubing flowing from his arm, to an attached bag of some kind of solution hanging on a metal hook at his side.

"Your dad's tough, and the hospital's not too far away. The doctors are expecting him. He'll be prepped for surgery immediately when we arrive," the medic said.

All Dustin could manage was a nod at the smiling woman. Betty hugged him close and stroked his back. The tears flowed freely. His defenses down from exhaustion, he closed his eyes and fell into a momentary oblivion.

The short escape lasted only a scattering of moments. Betty gently shook him. "We're here, Dustin. They're going to move us to a waiting room. The doctor sounded very optimistic that your father will have a full recovery. He's dehydrated and in shock from the loss of blood and his broken leg. They'll give us an update when he's out of surgery."

Not knowing what to say, and too tired to

attempt anything, he followed Betty to the waiting room. Dustin sat in a chair while Betty walked to the concession area and poured herself a cup of coffee.

The hours they waited seemed more like days. Every time a white coat appeared, they'd become alert, only to find the nurse walking by to the next nurse's station. He dozed when he could, but his mind wandered the dark depths of his soul. He'd awaken with a jerk, startling himself and Betty from the intensity.

Another hour passed. Betty paced the hallways, cup after cup of steaming coffee in hand, while Dustin glanced through magazines, not really seeing anything on the pages.

"Bill called to tell me he's on his way. One of the search teams will bring our horses and Tilly home, with the help of Steve and Carla. It seems Steve located the other mustangs in a ravine not far from where we found your father. Buck's a little beaten up, but overall, it sounds like all the mustangs are fine."

"I'm glad they were found." He was cut short by a nurse who stopped in front of them.

"I've good news for both of you. Mr. Collin's surgery was a success, and he's resting in the recovery room. He should be transferred to a room on the third floor in the next couple of hours. There, you'll be able to go in and see him for a short visit."

"Thank you, miss." Betty wiped a tear from her cheek. "That's excellent news."

The nurse moved on, and Betty hugged Dustin tight. It felt good to have strong arms around him, even if it wasn't his own mothers.

Bill arrived soon after the report from the nurse. Betty updated him on Trent's condition while Dustin walked the halls in search of a vending machine. It felt good to walk the kinks out of his body. He slid a dollar into the slot and pushed the button for a chocolate bar. He grabbed a cup of coffee on his way back to Betty and Bill. He could sure use the extra zing from the caffeine.

It took several more hours before the nurse returned and said his father could have a visitor. The three of them walked into the room together. Dustin's breath caught in his throat. It was difficult to see his father on that hospital bed, covered in tubes and obnoxious monitors beeping every few seconds. His father's eyes were still closed when they approached the bed. His face a ghoulish, pasty gray.

"Trent, you have visitors, sweetie. Dustin's here. He's a strong boy, just like you," Betty said aloud, pride thick in her voice.

Trent's eyelids fluttered, then opened. He tried to raise his hand, but it was covered in tubing, an IV attached to the vein in his hand.

"Dustin?" Trent's voice came out raspy.

Dustin rested his hand over his fathers. "I'm here, Dad."

Bill stepped closer to the bed. "Don't worry about talking right now, son. Take it easy. We just wanted to let you know we're all safe and here at your side. The horses are all fine. Dustin did a wonderful job of finding help for you. In fact, he's not even gotten any sleep yet. You go on and recuperate, and we'll make sure Dustin here does the same." Bill patted Trent on the shoulder.

His father tried to nod, causing him to grimace instead. He closed his eyes and his face relaxed.

"Dustin, Bill got us a hotel room not far from here. You and I will head on over there and rest. Bill will stay here with your father. Then, we'll come back first thing in the morning." Betty reached for his hand.

The thought of leaving his dad wasn't appealing, but he'd never been this exhausted in his life.

"All right," he said, turning with Betty. With a last glance at his dad, who now appeared peaceful in his sleep, he followed Betty out the door.

***

Dustin awoke with a start. Betty sat in a seat beside him, sipping from a styrofoam cup.

"I bought you a hot chocolate and a maple bar. We can leave to see your dad whenever you're ready."

He hopped out of bed. "I can eat on the way."

Betty chuckled. She rose from the chair and reached for her purse. "Let's go, cowboy."

Dustin liked the sound of that. He was pleased that Betty thought of him as a cowboy, like his dad.

The hospital was no less scary of a place than the day before. Their footsteps echoed on the tiles of the empty hallway leading to Trent's room. Why did his heart race so? All of the sudden his courage was depleted, and he wanted to run and hide, someplace safe. What did he fear? He knew exactly what it was. His father sending him back to his grandparents.

He could see it now. "I'm sorry, son, I can't have you living with me with my broken leg. You'll need to go back to your mother's family. The imaginary excuses raced through his mind. When they reached room sixteen, his father's room, he'd broken into a nervous sweat.

Bill stepped out of Trent's room.

"Howdy! All's well this morning. Dustin, I bet your dad would like to see you." Bill wore a wide grin on his face.

Bill walked over and wrapped Betty in an embrace. "Go on, son. He's waiting," he said over his shoulder.

Dustin took a deep breath to steady his nerves and stepped into the room, shutting the door behind him. He swallowed hard. A bedside lamp illuminated light across the room. The monitors attached to his dad still beeped and hummed. He walked past the nurse's workstation along the wall to his father's bed side.

"Morning, son," Trent said, his voice sounding stronger today.

"Dad..." Dustin was at a loss for words now. He stared at his father blankly. Last night, he'd had everything he hoped to say all planned out. Had all the reasons his father should let him stay at the ranch all firmly ingrained in his brain. Now, all those reasons were forgotten.

"I'm real proud of you. I hear you rode Scamp nonstop for help. Your actions saved my life."

"Dad—I don't want to go back. I don't want to leave you. I'm sorry for the horrible way I acted on the mountain." The tears streamed down his cheeks. He fell to his knees and buried his head into the side of the bed. A gentle touch tousled his hair.

"You don't have to go anywhere. I'd never send you back unless you wanted to go," Trent stated.

"I don't want to. Ever." Dustin looked up.

Trent cracked a smile. "Well I suppose it's settled then. You're staying."

"Best news I've heard," Bill concurred, walking into the room with Betty at his side. "Welcome to the family, kiddo."

CHAPTER FIFTEEN

Dustin pulled Scamp to a halt at the end of the meadow. He breathed deep, smiling as the breeze blew through his hair. Horse and boy faced the mountain. The same hills Scamp watched from his pasture each night. His previous home in the Ochoco's. Dark clouds rushed forward like an ocean wave over the ridge. A thunderstorm, he recognized, brewing and bubbling like a witch's cauldron and it was headed their way. Time to head back to the ranch.

Scamp trotted, tossing his head and prancing the whole way home. At the barn, Dustin made sure to curry the mustang till his coat shined and fed him an extra flake of hay with his dinner. Satisfied his horse was cozy and happy, he ducked his head from the rain and sprinted for the house, Tilly at his side.

Betty had a special dinner planned. It was a welcome home dinner for his father. Trent had been in the hospital three weeks now. There would still be a long road to recovery, but the doctors believed he'd be back in the saddle in no time.

Dustin reached the house the same time as Bill pulled up in his pickup truck. Betty stepped outside the ranch house, and grabbed the wheelchair parked by the front door and started wheeling it toward the truck's open door.

"Dad!" he greeted his father as Betty helped settle him into the wheelchair.

"Hi, looks like you've been out riding?"

"Yep, made it back to the barn right before this storm hit. I had Scamp out in the back pasture working on my riding skills."

"Nothing better than a quick jaunt out in the field before dinner," his dad remarked, a look of wistfulness on his face as he gazed toward the barn.

"Don't fret none, Trent. You'll be back in the saddle before you know it," Betty consoled him.

The night was filled with laughter and good food. Betty outdid herself with a feast of a pot roast with mashed potatoes, fresh baked rolls along with a peach cobbler baked in a Dutch oven over coals. For once, Dustin truly felt at home. Like he belonged with these people. His family.

"Before we settle Trent in his room for the night, we have a bit of news to share with you both."

Dustin and Trent looked at each other and shrugged before turning their attention back to Bill.

"Betty and I have done a lot of thinking these past few weeks. With the help of both of you, we'd like to extend our work with the mustangs. We'd like to turn the ranch into a place where folks can visit and learn about and work with the mustangs. A sort of equine therapy ranch you might say, for both children and adults alike. What do you boys say? Would you both be on board for something like this?"

"Of course! I think it's a wonderful idea," Trent said.

"How about you, Dustin?"

"I like the idea, too."

"That settles things then. We'll work out the details with time. Betty has a friend who has done this type of work in the past, and she offered to help get things started. But, there's no sense in rushing things. I'd like to see this be a successful endeavor," Bill said.

Betty wheeled Trent toward the spare room in the house where he'd be staying until he recouped. Dustin followed by his side. He placed a hand on his dad's shoulder. His father turned and smiled at him. At that moment, Dustin knew he was truly home. He still had questions for his father about the past, but for now, he was content with the way things were. Life with the Smith's and his dad, with mustangs and upcoming adventures on the horizon.

Glossary of Terms

Packhorse: Horse used to transport supplies

Pannier: Rectangular boxes of hard-plastic or canvas to evenly distribute supplies on an animal's back.

Highline: A length of rope stretched between two trees where you can tie your horse

Hobbles: Straps that link a horse's two front legs together

Leadline: Length of rope used to lead a horse

Three Strikes Mustang: Each time a mustang is offered for adoption and is passed over, it gets a strike. After three strikes, the BLM can sell the mustang 'without conditions' to anyone who agrees not to sell the mustang for slaughter.

Author Bio: L.B.Shire

L.B. Shire has been writing stories for as long as she can remember. She's always looking for a good horse story and if one can't be found, she makes one up herself.

When not writing or researching, L.B. enjoys spending time with family, spoiling her pampered pony, and, of course, reading anything that is set before her! She currently resides on the West Coast in a sleepy little mountain town. There, in the midst of all that beauty, she plans her characters' next adventures.

Printed in Great Britain
by Amazon

78670289R00072